Psycho Proctologists

and the

Flaming Buttholes of Doom

by W.W. Pecker

Psycho Proctologists and the Flaming Buttholes of Doom

Peckerhead Press

Copyright 2012 by W.W. Pecker

Psycho Proctologists
and the Flaming Buttholes of Doom

The man—or the demon inside the man . . . who could tell for sure?—emitted a chuckle that seemed more pitying than scornful. "Your faith is far too puny to vanquish me," it said. And the man smiled beatifically. "Weep, for my birth amidst the flames is nigh!"

And the burbling of his stomach rose to a crescendo. He closed his eyes, scrunched his face up in a rictus of concentration . . .

And farted a huge plume of green-tinged flame out his anus. I stared at it, my jaw dropping open in amazement. It was as if his anus had become the nozzle of some infernal flamethrower, and whatever roiled in his innards the accelerant.

The anal pyrotechnics eventually subsided, leaving a charred sulphury stench that permeated the entire dungeon.

In the silent aftermath of the demon's show of power, my own instinctive words rang out like an affront: *"What the fuuuuuck?"*

Psycho Proctologists

Author's Note

If I were inclined to dedicate this book to anyone (which I'm not—I mean, who would really want *this* book dedicated to them, anyway?), I'd dedicate it to all the guys who were there around the lunch table when "the conversation" took place. You know: one of *those* conversations. One where it gets so utterly ridiculous you can't believe you're actually having the conversation. If you have friends or relatives or colleagues with whom you have those types of conversations, consider yourself fortunate. And then run.

To writers, those types of conversations are the equivalent of a triple dog dare. Which just goes to show: watch what you say around a writer. You never know when they're actually going to *write* some of the crazy shit you say.

In all honesty, I don't think any of those people at the lunch table that day would remember "the conversation." I sincerely hope they don't, anyway, because then they would be in a position to out me. And if that happened . . . if it ever got back to my mother that I'd written this book . . . well, she'd go all *mothery* on me.

And that would really, really blow.

So if you're still reading this, I think I'll dedicate *Psycho Proctologists and the Flaming*

Buttholes of Doom to you, the stalwart few who are just psycho enough to keep reading past this point.

Psycho Proctologists and the Flaming Buttholes of Doom

is lovingly dedicated to

all the sick fucks of the world.

You know who you are.

W.W. Pecker

CHAPTER ONE

I was poking around in Kirk Cameron's ass when my intercom buzzed: three short buzzes in quick succession—my office's predetermined version of an SOS. *Shit.* Lousy timing for it.

Fortunately, Mr. Cameron was too preoccupied with my speculum up his ass to have noticed. "How does this feel, Mr. Cameron?" I asked him, using my best clinical tone, trying not to betray any hint of urgency. "Any pain?"

He shook his head. Bent over my examining table, his eyes closed, he wore a placid grin, as if I were his masseur and not his proctologist. "No . . . no, doc. That's . . . it's fine." I hadn't expected his answer to be any different from the last time, but I was still professionally bound to ask the question anyway.

I jiggled the speculum a little bit. "How about now?"

"No. No. Maybe . . . a little deeper?"

I sighed. I estimated I had at best a pair of minutes before the door to my examination room would burst open. Best to wrap this up quickly. So

I extracted the speculum. Kirk grunted as it came out.

"Everything looks just fine, Mr. Cameron," I told Kirk. "I don't see any warning signs at all."

Bent over my examining table, resting on his elbows, Kirk looked over his shoulder at me. His expression was crestfallen. "Nothing, doc? Are you sure you couldn't look a little deeper?"

I shook my head. "Everything's right as rain."

"Oh. I see."

"If you'll excuse me? I have to see to another patient. I believe you know where everything is?"

I left Kirk Cameron to wipe the lube off his ass. I exited my examination room, and fortunately intercepted my best friend Fister in the hallway about two point five seconds before he would have rushed right in on Kirk. I fixed Fister with my best glare. "What is it this time?" I asked. I took him by the elbow and steered him down the hallway back in the direction of my waiting room.

Fister—Joseph H. Fitz, Jr., to be precise, but ever since we were kids I'd called him by his nickname—was fit to bursting with enthusiasm. "You've gotta come with me," he said. "I—you won't believe it. It's . . . it's . . ."

I sighed. "Fister, you know I'd love to, but I just don't have time. I've got a full schedule of appointments this afternoon." Which was a huge fib; I'd cleared the entire afternoon for Kirk Cameron, as usual.

"But—" Fister took a deep breath, but at that moment was distracted by the sight of Kirk Cameron emerging from the examination room at the back end of the hall. Kirk was wearing his dark sunglasses, and his head was bowed— "is that . . .?"

Before Fister could finish his sentence, I shoved him into an unused examination room and closed the door.

"—Kirk Cameron?" Fister finished.

"I'm a physician," I said. "My client list is confidential."

Fister frowned at me. "I thought he stopped seeing you over a year ago."

I said nothing. I merely looked over the top of my glasses at Fister in an attempt to tell him to drop it—which of course was the wrong tack exactly with Fister. I should have known better; I'd known him for twenty years, after all.

Fister's boyish face broke out in a devilish grin. He chortled—he actually chortled. I'd never heard anybody chortle like Fister. "You know you've totally sold out, haven't you? I mean, come on . . . Kirk Cameron?"

"I'm ethically bound not to discuss my clients with you."

"You know you're totally his bitch, right? There's nothing wrong with his ass. There never has been."

"So now you're capable of making a diagnosis without ever having examined a patient?" Fister was a board certified proctologist, like me, but even he wasn't that good.

Fister hooted. "You know he just comes here so you'll stick things up his ass, right? If he wasn't such an uptight fuckwad, he could stick things up his own ass. Have you told him that?"

I scowled. The thought had actually crossed my mind . . . but Kirk Cameron was my best customer, especially ever since Richard Gere had joined PETA.

"Did you write him a prescription? How about a nice giant-sized dildo twice daily until the inflammation of his ego subsides?"

"A dildo is not a medically sound . . ."

"Or maybe a leather fetish gangbang? I bet a dozen or so bears' cocks up his hole would cure his case of rectal itch real fast."

"Fister . . ."

"Or have you suggested fisting? He might even find Jesus for real if he tried it just once."

"I—"

Fister cackled with glee. "Now I know how you're financing this fancy office and your shiny new car. You know he just comes here to get his jollies every week. Is that—" He sketched air quotes. "—medically ethical? You know if he could just bring himself to ride a dick like every other closet case you'd never have to see him again. You could cure him, Mikey." Fister put his hand on my shoulder and adopted a somber air, like a pedant schooling a wayward pupil. "You could do more than that, Mikey. You could spare the world some bullshit. Oh, so much bullshit." Fister was working his way up to his best imitation of a televangelist. "Just think about it. You could make the world a better place for closeted fairies everywhere. You could save the world, Mikey! Can I get a hallelujah?"

"I'm a doctor, not a psychologist."

"Oh ye of little faith . . ."

"All right," I said resignedly. I knew he'd drop the subject of my ongoing treatment of Kirk Cameron's imagined rectal maladies if I agreed to go with him on whatever wild snipe hunt he'd fallen into this week. "I'll go with you."

"You're a pal, Mikey. You're a real pal. You know that, right?"

Fister knew where we were going, so we took his dilapidated Ford Probe across town, to a spot near Mann's Chinese Theater. Fister's car was a mess: the back bumper drooped from a rear-ending he'd suffered a few months ago that he'd never bothered to get fixed, and the right rear tail light was smashed in. Every time I climbed into Fister's passenger seat I fretted the whole way that at any moment we might see the flashing lights of a police cruiser in the rearview mirror, but for some reason the L.A. cops always let Fister pass unmolested.

Not that his interior was much to write home about, either. The back seat hosted a graveyard of old Burger King sandwich wrappers (Fister hated hamburgers, but absolutely loved breakfast croissanwiches), and as I was climbing into the car I even spotted a condom wrapper, and I wondered how long it had been since Fister'd had it his way in his back seat. He was a romantic, for sure.

I focused on inhaling his pine-scented air freshener for most of the ride across town in order to take the edge off the myriad other aromas that mingled together in his car. Fister didn't speak the whole way, and I knew better than to engage him in conversation. But when he pulled the car into a parking spot in front of a Starbucks in the neighborhood of Las Palmas and Franklin, I raised an eyebrow. "I thought you hated Starbucks," I said. In fact, Fister had spent a good three months last year testing a hypothesis and arriving at the conclusion that Starbucks' macchiatos increased flatulence by 17.3%. I hadn't bothered to ask him to show me his data—or exactly how he'd gone about testing his hypothesis. I didn't really want to know.

Fister didn't answer. Instead, he leaned over my lap and rummaged in his glove box. He pulled out a pair of latex gloves which he shoved in his jacket pocket, followed by a crucifix and a small green Gideon's Bible—the pocket version.

"What the fuck, Fisty?" I said. "Since when did you get religion?"

Still bent over my lap, he turned his head and grinned up at me. "When in Rome, you've gotta play the part," he said. And he pulled one more thing out of the glove box: a white collar insert. He straightened up and fastened it under his collar in the rearview mirror. With his black button-down shirt, he made for a passable imitation of a priest.

"Are you crazy?" I said. "You're not even Catholic."

"I've been studying up on it," he said.

"You mean you actually read some of that Bible?"

"Of course not. I fucked a choirboy, and then

felt really really bad about it. What else is there to know? Come on."

I followed Fister out of the car and into the Starbucks. I hoped he was joking about the choirboy. With Fister, you never knew.

The espresso-scented invigoration of a Starbucks high greeted me as I entered the coffee shop after Fister. I inhaled deeply, but Fister was already on the move. He nodded cordially to the pair of pimply-faced baristas behind the counter and headed toward the back door that read EMPLOYEES ONLY.

Fister led me into a storeroom laced with bags of coffee. At the far end of the storeroom was another door. Fister strode straight toward it and pulled it open.

That door led us into a long, narrow corridor lit only by a bare forty-watt incandescent bulb that cast shadows over the entire corridor. At the end of it, a lone door, half-cracked, awaited us like an invitation. *Come into my parlor.* I thought, and shuddered. Somehow, we'd gone from Starbucks to Shelob's lair in two point six seconds. "Fisty, what the hell is this place?" I whispered. I don't know why the hell I was whispering; it wasn't a library, and there wasn't anyone around.

Fister didn't reply in kind. He answered in a normal, conversational tone that felt like a sacrilege as he strode down the dimly lit corridor toward the door at the end. "The shop fronts an old warehouse," he said. "The Leather and Lattes Meetup meets here the second Tuesday of every month."

"Leather and Lattes?" I muttered, grimacing.

"Hey, don't knock it till you tried it," Fister said. "You'd be amazed at the palliative effects of a macchiato foam rimjob."

I followed Fister through the open door at the end of the corridor, and we emerged into a dimly lit underground warehouse chamber with redbrick walls and a low ceiling. The place was decked out in leather dungeon decor: chain harnesses hung from the ceiling, and the floor was furnished with about a half a dozen wooden racks in various shapes and sizes. Against the wall was a rack of implements: studded collars, shock rods, specula that would've made Kirk Cameron's eyes light up like a kid in a candy store, enema cans, and more items I couldn't quite identify, much less imagine how to use.

In the center of the chamber, naked, legs up in the stirrups, was the patient we'd come to see, I assumed. He was a forty-something man with balding strawberry blond hair, but in rather trim shape. Put a pair of glasses on him and he could be an accountant by day, leather daddy by night.

A young woman, maybe mid-twenties, dressed in a slave collar and a Catholic schoolgirl outfit stood over him. She was too old to be a real Catholic schoolgirl, unless she'd flunked about a half-dozen grades, but judging by the skirt that barely covered the lower parts of her cheeks, I gathered that the outfit wasn't really nun-approved. She moved to greet us as we entered. "Oh, Father, thank goodness you've come," she said to Fister. She'd apparently been crying; her black mascara streaked dirty smudges down her cheeks, making her look like Alice Cooper. And her relief at seeing Fister seemed genuine enough: she threw her arms around him and buried her face on his shoulder.

"Of course, my child," Fister said. "God would not abandon you in your hour of need." With one hand he patted her shoulder, and with the other he reached around and patted her rump.

She broke the embrace and stood back. She looked to me.

"This is my assistant," Fister introduced me, "Father McLovin." He shot me a sly wink.

The woman accorded me a nod. "Thank you for coming, father," she said. Then, she addressed both Fister and me. "Please, can you help my daddy?"

She took Fister's hand and led him closer to the man spreadeagled in the harness. I followed a few steps behind, wondering if the man in the harness were actually her father, or if 'daddy' was just a fetishist's honorific.

Fister immediately was at his most clinical. He'd never even gone through the motions of setting up a practice; after getting through his residency and getting his bona fides, he'd always been content to rely on his sizable trust fund which enabled him to bounce from one crazy half-assed (if you'll pardon the pun) preoccupation to the next. It appeared to me as if sadomasochism and impersonating a Catholic priest was his latest fad. But as I watched him circle around to stand over the patient's shoulder and look down at the naked daddy, who appeared to be sleeping, I couldn't help but be impressed at the clinician Fister always could have become.

"How long has he been like this?" Fister asked the young woman.

"About a day and a half," the girl said. "It's . . . it's awful, father."

As if on cue, the man's eyes snapped open. Laid out as he was in the harness, the man stared straight up at the ceiling for a moment, not focusing on anything in particular. Standing over Fister's shoulder, I took a step back: the man's eyes weren't right. They were deep black, and seemed to be lacking any whites. I must have gasped, because Fister laid a reassuring hand on my shoulder.

The man's creepy eyes moved then. They focused on Fister, and then me beside him. An involuntary shudder wracked my body; I couldn't help it.

And then the man smiled. It was a creepy, sneering smile that seemed to suck all the humor out of the cosmos. "How good of you to come, Father," he said to Fister. His voice was creaky and gravelly and scratchy all at the same time, as if a demonic bullfrog had taken up residence in his larynx. And then he laughed, long and loud and derisive. "Though I dare say you're no priest." He laughed again, though this time more of a rumbling Mephistophelian chuckle at some private joke.

This man didn't need a priest, I thought. He needed an optometrist . . . and quite possibly a shrink.

But a moment later I rethought my opinion. As I looked down at him, his stomach rumbled audibly, a deep burbly belchy sound that reverberated in the dungeon, and it was matched by the flesh on his stomach rippling and rolling in undulating waves, as if some creature were tunneling around in his innards. My eyes widened.

Fister seemed unfazed, though. He calmly reached into his jacket and pulled out his Gideon's Bible from his pocket. He held it in his right hand, and with his left he pulled out a sheet of paper. "Actually, I am a priest," he said. He extended the piece of paper toward the man's face. I looked questioningly at Fister; in response, he flashed me his schoolboy grin. "Ordained by internet just this morning."

The man looked at the paper, and a hearty, withering guffaw erupted from his chest. "Episcopalian?" he said. "Pussy."

Fister didn't seem perturbed in the slightest. "I'm minister enough to send your ass back to hell, demon!" he cried. And he tossed the Bible to me. "Read something."

I stared at him. I hadn't even touched a Bible since an ill-fated trip to summer camp when I was twelve and my parents had wanted to get rid of me for a few weeks. "But—" I said. "—I don't . . . what should I read?"

"It doesn't matter. Just read something."

I responded to the tone of command in Fister's voice. I opened the Bible and began to read. "And it came to pass after these things, that his master's wife cast her eyes upon Joseph; and she said, 'Lie with me.' But he refused, and said unto his master's wife, Behold, my master wotteth not what is with me in the house, and he hath committed all that he hath to my hand; There is none greater in this house than I; neither hath he kept back any thing from me but thee, because thou art his wife . . ."

I trailed off when I realized both Fister and the young woman were looking at me, frowning. "Not that," Fister said. "Read something else."

I flipped further back in the book and opened to a random page. I picked out a verse at random: "And John answered him, saying, Master, we saw one casting out devils in thy name, and he followeth not us: and we forbad him, because he followeth not us. But Jesus said, Forbid him not: for there is no man which shall do a miracle in my name, that can lightly speak evil of me."

"Now we're talking!" Fister said gleefully. He held his hands out toward the man in the harness and crossed his index fingers in the sign of the cross. "*Get out, demon!*" he commanded. "In the name of the Father, the Son, and the . . ." He mumbled something incomprehensible; I could tell he had no earthly idea what the third element of the Trinity was. "I command you to leave this man's body!"

The demon inside the naked man didn't seem to be impressed. "It's the Holy Spirit, fuckwad," he said.

"Yeah yeah, whatever," Fister said. "Just get the fuck out."

After the last several Satanic laughs that had seemed to express contempt for the entire universe, the man—or the demon inside the man . . . who could tell for sure?—emitted a chuckle that seemed more pitying than scornful. "Your faith is far too puny to vanquish me," it said. And the man smiled beatifically. "Weep, for my birth amidst the flames is nigh!"

And the burbling of his stomach rose to a crescendo. He closed his eyes, scrunched his face up in a rictus of concentration . . .

And farted a huge plume of green-tinged flame out his anus. I stared at it, my jaw dropping open in amazement. It was as if his anus had become the nozzle of some infernal flamethrower, and whatever roiled in his innards the accelerant.

The anal pyrotechnics eventually subsided, leaving a charred sulphury stench that permeated the entire dungeon.

In the silent aftermath of the demon's show of power, my own instinctive words rang out like an affront: *"What the fuuuuuck?"*

The words hung there in the air a moment. An eerie silence hung over the dungeon; it was broken a moment later by some single, semi-silent hiccupping sob from the young woman.

Fister patted her on the shoulder. "Don't worry, my dear. We're not quite out of tricks yet." I thought it quite kind of him to include me as part of his reassurance—assuming, of course, that he wasn't just employing a royal *we* (with Fister you could never really tell)—because I certainly was plum out of tricks myself. Left to my own devices—and if the naked man in the sling hadn't been blocking my path to the door—I'd have been halfway back to the parking lot by now. I could have remained skeptical about the whole demonic possession schtick, blackened pupils and everything, but anal pyrotechnics on the level I'd just witnessed were hard to fake.

Fister reached inside his jacket pocket and pulled out a large crucifix. I raised an eyebrow, because crucifixes weren't Fister's style at all, but then I realized that this was a crucifix with something extra. It was fashioned out of rubber, and the bottom end of it opposite the crossbars of the cross was shaped in the bulbous shape of a penis head. As dildos were concerned, this one certainly wasn't the oddest I've ever seen (I pull things out of people's asses for a living, after all), but it certainly scored points as the most sacrilegious. Or the most religious, depending upon your point of view. I thought Kirk Cameron certainly might have found being penetrated by it to be a deeply religious experience.

It wasn't for the casual bottom, that much was certain. In diameter it was about as big around as a soda can, and in length nearly twice as long as that. At the sight of it, the naked man's black, pupil-less eyes widened, and the first glimmerings of unease flickered on his face. But only for a moment—a second later the casual derision of the demon possessing him returned. "You think that will be enough?" he scoffed.

"Maybe not," Fister said. He reached inside his jacket pocket again and withdrew a tiny vial of something. "Here," he said to me, and thrust the dildo into my hands. "Hold this for a second."

I fumbled with the dildo, not quite sure how

exactly to hold it. Grasping it by the shaft didn't quite seem appropriate, but I couldn't quite keep a grip on it any other way, so I swallowed my knee-jerk reaction and grasped it firmly, wrapping both hands between the crossbars of the cross and the bulbous penis head at the bottom. Then, for good measure, I swiveled it around to hold it protectively between myself and the demon-possessed man. If he'd scoffed at the puniness of Fister's faith, I was certain he'd break into fits of hysterics at being confronted with mine.

But he wasn't paying any attention to me at all. His funky-assed eyes were focused on Fister, who was unscrewing the stopper on his vial. He drew out a dropper, then stuck out his hand to me as if to request the dildo back. I was only too happy to hand it over.

"You may think my faith is puny," Fister said, "but that of the man who gave me this was unwavering." He squeezed the rubber tip of the dropper, and a clear liquid dribbled out onto the head of the dildo. I opened my mouth to ask Fister just what the hell was in the vial, but then quickly closed my mouth again. I didn't really want to know that badly.

Fister lubed up the head of the dildo and the shaft, rubbing the clear liquid into it until the rubber shone with a wet sheen. Then, he brandished the dildo and bent over to apply it to the demon-possessed man's anus.

Before he could, the young woman in the schoolgirl outfit stopped him with a hand on his shoulder. "Be careful, Father," she said. "He—

it . . . he'll burn you."

"Yes yes yes!" the man in the sling cackled maniacally. "You'll burn, you'll burn, you'll burn, *motherfucker*! Come into my parlor if you dare!" And he collapsed into peals of giggles that sent ripples of gooseflesh along my arms.

It was Fister's turn to look uneasy then, as if he really weren't relishing the prospect of getting so near the blast zone, but he took a deep breath to steel his resolve. "I'll be fine, my dear," he said. And then he turned to me. "Read," he said.

I stared at him. "Huh?"

"Read." He motioned to the little version of the Bible I still held in my left hand. "It'll distract him."

I opened the Bible to a random page and started to read. "And Isaac begat Jacob, and Jacob begat Judas and his brothers . . ." God, that was fucking lame. I quickly flipped to another page.

"Louder," Fister said. "Read it like you mean it."

I finally found a decent page and started reading the first verse I found. "'Yet it pleased the lord to bruise him; he hath put him to grief: when thou shalt make his soul an offering for sin, he shall see his seed, he shall prolong his days, and the pleasure of the lord shall prosper in his hand.'"

While I read, I kept one eye on Fister. He bent down over the possessed man and positioned the specially lubricated dildo at his orifice. At the merest touch of the dildo's head against his anus, the man spasmed once, a massive full-body flinch that caused me to respond in kind. I instinctively took a step backward.

Fister didn't stop there. He twisted the head of the dildo, like a man trying to screw a light bulb into a socket where it didn't really fit. As he worked the dildo's tip into the orifice, the man in the sling started to buck violently, and he screeched in a mixture of rage and pain.

"Hold him!" Fister instructed. I stopped reading the scripture verse I was on for a moment, thinking he was talking to me, but then I realized he was talking to the young woman in the schoolgirl outfit. She complied by leaning over the man's midriff and pressing down on his hips so Fister could continue.

Unbidden, my eyes flicked to the man's stomach. It was roiling again in that way that was just so unfucking natural, like the undulating of a wave on the ocean, and I knew that the demon inside him was cooking up another anal blast to rival the first. And that Fister was right in his crosshairs.

"Read!" Fister bellowed.

I cleared my throat, and then delved back into the book I held in my hands. ". . .

Behold, thou desirest truth in the inward parts: and in the hidden part thou shalt make me to know wisdom."

I partitioned off my perception: part of me focused on the words on the page so that I could read them aloud and keep some semblance of authority in my voice (it was all feigned, but what the hell?), and the other kept a stray eye on Fister's progress. He now had the dildo's head firmly inserted and was slowly working the shaft millimeter by millimeter up the possessed man's stretched orifice. The man—or the demon inside; it was hard to tell which—reacted by bucking and thrashing violently in his sling. It was fortunate that he was handcuffed and ankle-cuffed into position, or he'd never have been still enough for Fister to find a point of entry. At the same time the demon, through the conduit of the man's voice, screamed what I assumed were horrible things at Fister in a language I couldn't understand or even place. The man's blackened pupils were now tinged with a fiery red glow that radiated fury.

And all the while, the man's stomach inflated like a soufflé rising in the oven, rising like a bubble, rising, rising . . .

"Um, Fister . . ." I muttered.

"Almost there," Fister said. His tongue stuck out a fraction at the right corner of his mouth between his tightly clenched teeth, an expression I recognized as his token air of concentration, and beads of sweat stood out on his forehead.

"I think you'd better hurry," I said in between verses of Revelations.

Fister straightened up just long enough to stare at the enormous gas bubble rising in the man's stomach. His eyes widened to match the dilation of the possessed man's sphincter. And only a second later I saw his resolve harden. "Sorry about this," he muttered to the man in the sling. He gripped the crossbeams of the crucifix dildo and shoved.

The demon inside the possessed man shrieked, an eardrum-rupturing banshee wail of agony and hate. It paused only long enough for the man it inhabited to draw breath. Then, its eyes flared completely red, and they focused down the length of the man's torso on Fister, who was still firmly in his sights between his legs. "My master will come, and he will have his revenge on you!" he cried. "He will have his revenge on all of humanity!"

And then he blew. The green-tinged flames sprayed out of his aperture, launching the dildo like a missile. It struck the brick wall across the room with enough force to blast a chunk of brick out of the wall. The demon-fueled stream of hellfire continued for several seconds, bathing everything in the dungeon in its unnatural glow. I couldn't help myself: I dove for cover and shielded my eyes, even though I was outside the blast radius.

Finally, the flames subsided. The man in the sling gave one last grunting sigh, and his head lolled to the side. He was unconscious.

I needed a few moments to regain my feet. The air stank of sulfur and feces and more awful scents I was too stunned to identify. I struggled to keep down my gorge even as I stumbled nearer to the man in the sling. "Fister?" I called. My voice croaked out.

No answer.

"Fister?" I called again, my voice slightly stronger this time.

As I came to look at the space between the man's spreadeagled legs, I saw Fister. His hair was charred, but to my great relief he was slowly climbing back to his feet. He looked slightly dazed, but at the same time he wore his trademark little-boy grin. And then he chuckled. "I did it," he said, as if he couldn't quite believe it himself.

Fister ducked underneath the man's elevated left leg. He located the schoolgirl, who'd dived for cover just as I had. He helped her to her feet and steadied her as she regained her bearings. "Are you all right, my dear?" he asked.

At length, she nodded. Fister took her by the hand and led her back toward the unconscious body of her daddy in the sling.

"Is he . . . is he . . .?"

Fister bent over the man. First he checked his pulse at his neck, then he opened the man's eyelids. I was relieved to see that his eyes were now normal again, with pupils and pale green irises.

"He'll be fine now," Fister said. And he patted the young woman in the schoolgirl outfit on the rump. "Everything's going to be okay now."

The girl collapsed in sobs of relief on Fister's shoulder. "Oh, thank you, thank you, Father!"

Fister let her sob for a moment, then extricated himself from her embrace. Looking somewhat smug and self-satisfied, he surveyed the dungeon. His gaze lingered from a second on the crucifix dildo still quivering where it was embedded in the wall. He sketched a hasty sign of the cross. Then, he turned to me and said, "Well. I think our work here is finished."

He strode over to me and nudged me back toward the dungeon's entrance. We left, back down the long tunnel we'd come down to enter here.

As we entered the Starbucks, leaving the stench of burnt sulfur behind for the aromas of macchiatos and espresso, I asked Fister, "What was that you put on the . . . on the . . ." I couldn't quite bring myself to say the word *dildo* out loud. Not in public.

Fister grinned at me. "The seed of an archbishop. Very rare. Very valuable."

I frowned. "How the hell did you come by the seed of an archbishop?"

He shrugged. "Ebay. How else? But don't ask me what he got off to."

CHAPTER TWO

Neither of us spoke all the way to the parking lot, and even when I got back within the comforting confines of Fister's old clunker, all I could do while he wrestled with the ignition, put the car in gear, and tore out of the Starbucks parking lot was to stare through the passenger side window, blinking stupidly.

Finally, as Fister pulled us onto the highway, I mastered my vocal chords enough to say, "So this is what you've been doing for the past year and a half?"

Fister nodded. "Give or take a decade or so."

"A decade? You've been doing this since med school, then?"

"Yeah."

"And you never told me?"

Fister shrugged. I was thankful he was driving and I was in the passenger seat; the arrangement spared us the awkwardness of having to make eye contact. "You never would have believed me."

I opened my mouth, then closed it again quickly. Whatever retort I might have made died in the cold hard light of his honesty. He was right. There's no way I would have ever believed any of the things I'd just witnessed . . .

But now . . .

"Was that . . . that was a real demon, wasn't it?"

Fister nodded. "Of the Parahelix Assumptive variety."

I blinked. "The what?"

"The name's not important. There are lots and lots of types of demons."

"Oh. Of course." *There would have to be, wouldn't there*? I didn't verbalize.

"The Parahelix Assumptive are just your garden variety demons. They're pretty badass if they manage to cross all the way over into our plane of existence, but most of the time the best they can manage is a token possession here and there. Fortunately they're particularly susceptible to Catholic iconography."

"I see," I said, as if he were merely telling me it was going to rain today. "So does that mean that not all demons are as easily vanquished by crucifixes and archbishops' semen?"

"I'm afraid not. In the demon world, there's some really nasty motherfuckers out there."

I shivered a little, despite the heat of the day and Fister's sputtery, half-functional air conditioning. And I fervently hoped Fister didn't mean what he'd just said literally.

"And you . . . you . . ." I didn't really have the words to have this conversation, but I stumbled forth anyway. "You do this all the time? You fight these demons?"

Fister looked sheepish. "Not really. This was my first, actually." He grinned. "I wanted you to be there when I popped my cherry. It seemed only fitting."

I was oddly touched. I'd been there when Fister had popped his real cherry sixteen years ago in the back seat of my car. I'd had to be; I was sixteen and Fister was fifteen, and he couldn't legally drive by himself, so I'd had to be the chauffeur for his date. They'd both magnanimously invited me to participate with them, but I'd left them to it and went and bought popcorn instead. And disinfectant.

"So . . ." I said then. "What now?"

"We should go get a drink to celebrate," Fister said. He reached over and punched me playfully on the arm. "We just kicked a demon's ass and it's not even noon yet. How many people can say that, eh?"

I shrugged. "Not many. I sincerely hope, anyway."

Fister grinned, and he took his eyes off the road long enough to look over at me. He reached out and patted my cheek affectionately. "You were magnificent, by the way. You read those verses with such authority. You almost fooled me into thinking you were a priest."

I couldn't help but return his grin: his enthusiasm was infectious; it always was. "Altar boys of the world, look out," I said.

A companionable silence passed between us. I watched as Fister approached the exit that would head back to my office. He passed it by. I turned to him. "Um, Fister—"

Fister wasn't paying me any attention. His eyes were focused on something in his rearview mirror. "We're being followed," he said.

"We're—what?" I shifted in my seat to look out the rear windshield—

"Don't turn around," Fister said. "We don't want him to know we know he's there."

"He—who is 'he?' Fisty, I don't understand. What's—"

"Take a look in the passenger side mirror. Casual-like, though."

I did as he instructed. I peered as closely as I could while still trying to look as if I were doing nothing more than glancing casually in the passenger side mirror. "I don't see anything," I said.

At that moment Fister made a quick lane change. He ignored the angry honk and the finger from the driver he cut off. "There," he said. "You see it?"

"See what?"

"Two cars back. Every time I change lanes, the black Azera changes lanes with me. Every time I speed up, it keeps up with me. Every time I slow down, he slows down too so he's always two cars behind me."

"I don't understand. Who is 'he?'"

"How the hell should I know?" Fister said. "I can't exactly get out of the car and ask him."

"Well, why would somebody be following you?"

"I don't know. Let's find out." Fister flashed me his best rakish grin. "Hold onto your butt."

And he pressed his foot all the way down on the accelerator. His beater struggled and lurched into the next gear. Fister kept his foot on the gas pedal until he was doing in excess of ninety-five miles per hour, and then he made three lane changes in quick succession.

I peered into the passenger side mirror. I still hadn't spotted the black Azera that Fister claimed was there—but then, I generally paid no attention to cars, and wouldn't know a Azera from a Volkswagen from a BMW.

"Damn. Still there."

Fister made another lane change. We came upon the next exit, and were nearly past it when Fister yanked on the steering wheel. We shot over to the right and onto the exit ramp at the last possible second. And then I saw it: two cars back, a black vehicle repeated the same maneuver. No doubt about it now. Somebody *was* following us.

Once off the Interstate, I braced myself for a Keanu Reeves-style romp through residential districts and commercial districts. But instead, Fister slowed down, and started driving like a geriatric out for a Sunday drive.

And the car followed us.

"You didn't lose him," I told Fister.

"I wasn't trying to lose him." Fister grinned. "I was just fucking with him. Letting him know that I know that he's following me."

"Great," I said. "So now what are you gonna do?"

Fister shrugged. "Piss him off, I guess." Fister slowed down even further, until he was driving well under the speed limit. We were heading toward Venice, just outside of Santa Monica, and Fister angled toward the beaches. I thought his plan was probably a good one: head toward where the most people would be, use the population as a shield so that whoever was following us would be hard pressed to start shooting.

Or at least that's what I thought Fister's plan was. At least until he brought his Probe into the parking lots of a public park, parked, and turned off the ignition. "What are you doing?" I cried, and my voice came out a little high-pitched and hysterical.

"I figure this is about as good a place as any to find out what he wants," Fister said. "Fancy a stroll in thepark? Nice day for it."

"You're just going to get out and go for a stroll when there could be a demon following you?"

"A demon? Where on earth did you get that idea?"

"I—I just . . ." I halted my stammering. "I just thought . . ."

"Demons don't need to drive cars. If a demon wanted to kill us, we'd probably be dead by now."

"Oh. That's . . . cheering."

"No," Fister continued as if lecturing a child, "this is probably one of their earthly minions."

"Their what?"

"The fuckholes who like to conjure demons."

"Oh. Why would one of them be following us?"

Fister grinned. "Probably for revenge. We did just kick a Parahelix Assumptive's ass, you know."

"Oh."

I didn't have much more time for a lesson in demonology. Fister blithely got out of the driver's side and locked his door. His Probe was actually so old and so cheap that he had to physically lock the door with the key. I wrestled with whether to follow him or not; I wasn't sure I saw the logic of going out into the open park with a pissed-off demon conjurer on our tails . . . but then, I didn't really want to make a target of myself by sitting in a car all by myself, either. So I lumbered out of the car and caught up to Fister, who was already strolling across the park.

It was a beautiful day. Mothers with strollers were out in force, as were lycra-clad joggers and speed walkers and even roller bladers taking advantage of the park's paved paths. I thought Fister's strategy of sticking to well-peopled areas until maybe our trail lost interest in us might have been a good one, until Fister started to angle toward shadier, lesser used areas of the park. "Um, Fister—" I said. I cast a look over my shoulder and tried to make it look casual, like I wasn't *trying* to look over my shoulder.

Fister ignored me. We came to a park bathroom nestled in one corner of the park. Fister entered, and I reluctantly followed. Maybe Fister had a plan . . . maybe. If he did, I tried to figure out what it might be, because I thought it probably sucked. We were heading into a deserted area and cutting off our every avenue of retreat. Unless, of course, Fister was meaning to make his stand in the bathroom . . . stake out our territory and force our assailant to come into our parlor . . . not a bad strategy, but foolhardy, unless Fister had come by some fighting skills that I never knew he had. Whatever his plan, I hoped he wasn't counting on me for backup.

I ducked into the bathroom right behind Fister. The smell of urinal cakes overlaid with the strong stench of piss greeted my nostrils. As soon as the graffitied spring-swinging door clanged shut, I whispered to Fister, "So what's your plan?"

Fister looked at me quizzically. "I plan on laying a deuce. If you'll excuse me." And he staked out one of the stalls and closed the door.

I stood there for a moment, feeling completely out of my depth. Demons and demon conjurers were far beyond my ken.

Nothing happened. My heart thumped a thumpa-thumpa beat in my chest, but none of the scenarios in my imagination transpired: no ninjas burst through the door wielding throwing stars to bury in my chest, no horned demons spun into existence from the urinal drains . . .

And I did have to pee. Rather urgently. It was probably my bladder's reaction to panic; it always behaved thusly. Even as a jittery pre-adolescent, the moment before I had to step on stage for piano recitals, I'd always had to piss.

So I walked over to the urinal, unfastened my fly, and let loose.

And at that moment the bathroom door *screeeeeed* open. Startled, I jumped, and leaked a few drops of urine onto my right hand.

I was caught in a compromising position. Still in mid-piss, I couldn't quite turn around to see my would-be assailant . . .

No matter, though. A moment later a beefy blond man in biker shorts and a tank top appeared at the urinal next to me. I glanced over at him, and he glanced over at me. He smiled and gave me a casual nod. I focused on completing my business; odd, I know, but it was completely rational to me. If a demon conjurer was going to kill me, I was at least going to go out of this world with enough dignity not to piss myself.

But he didn't appear interested in killing me at all. Instead, he unzipped himself and set about his business. All too soon, he started jiggling.

I frowned. My stream was tapering off; I was just about at the jiggling stage. He'd just arrived; he couldn't be ready for jiggling yet. I looked over at him. He returned my glance with a nod and a smile bigger yet than the first one he'd flashed me. And he jiggled harder.

I raised an eyebrow. *Oh shit.*

Now with an incentive to get the hell out of there, I jiggled the last drops of piss off my junk and started to zip up.

And just as I was doing so, I felt something pinch my butt left butt cheek. I yelped a little; I couldn't help it. The man to my left responded by chuckling softly. "It's all right," he whispered. "You don't have to be nervous. I'm not a cop."

"You're—you're not—I mean—you're not a demon conjurer?" I sputtered out.

The man looked a little nonplussed, but his smile never faltered. Nor did his jiggling. "I can be if you want me to be," he said.,

"Um, no, that's all right." I buried myself in my underwear and zipped up. "I think I'd better go." I retreated across the bathroom, paused just long enough to see that Fister was going to be no help—beneath the door of the stall, I saw that his pants were around his ankles, and he was grunting slightly from exertion.

I wasn't thinking. I withdrew, back out into the sunlight of a Los Angeles day—

—and found a knife tip at my throat. A pissed-looking woman, maybe mid-thirties, with fiery red curly hair, was on the other end of it. She held the blade at my throat. I was trapped.

Shit.

"Come out nice and slow," she told me. "Hands up."

I did as she instructed. What choice did I have? I could have tried to retreat back into the men's room, but if I tried that she could have buried the knife in any of half a dozen painful locations around my body. So I shuffled a few steps away from the door, my hands up in the air like a pussified T-Rex. She backed me up against the wall of the building.

"Who are you?" she demanded. "Why are you conjuring demons?"

"I—what?" My voice cracked like an adolescent boy. I took a deep breath and managed to say, "I—we weren't conjuring demons. We were—um—"

"What?"

"We . . ." What the hell was the right word? "We . . . vanquished one." I cringed inwardly. Put that way, what Fister and I had done this morning sounded so pompous.

She sized me up in disbelief. "You? You vanquished a demon?"

I nodded. "Of the Parahelix Assymptote variety."

She rolled her eyes. "Amateurs." She considered for a second. She didn't let up the pressure on her knifepoint, but at least she didn't drive it any deeper into the soft flesh of my throat, either. "Say it," she said at length.

I could only look at her helplessly. "Say what?"

She rolled her eyes again. "In darkest hour . . ." she prompted.

"I—"

"You're lying."

"I'm not lying!"

"Then say it!"

"Say what?" I was thankful I'd just gone to the bathroom, because otherwise I'd be wetting myself. "I don't know—"

"In darkest hour . . ." She said again.

Fuck. Where the hell was Fister?

When I didn't say anything, she pressed harder on the tip of her blade.

"In darkest hour . . ." I said. I mumbled something incoherent, like you'd do when you were trying to mimic speaking a foreign language that you really didn't speak. ". . . Green Lantern's power," I finished

She hesitated for a moment, and then relaxed her grip. She pulled the knife away from my throat, but she still kept it raised so that I would be easily pokeable with it. "You're either a really good liar, or one sorry-assed motherfucker," she said. "So you wanna tell me how you managed to vanquish a Parahelix Assumptive?"

"Um . . . Archbishop sperm," I said.

The answer satisfied her enough to back off a pace. She still looked pissed off, but her scowl was fading. She nodded to the bathroom door a few paces to my right. "Tell me about your friends."

"Friends?"

"The two who went in there with you."

"Um—actually, only one of them is my friend."

"You pick up random tricks in the park, then?"

"What? No!"

"Hey, no judgment. We've all done it once or twice. So who's your friend?"

"Um . . . you mean Fister?"

"I don't care what you two do together. Just tell me his name."

At that moment the screechy spring-door of the men's room creaked open. The blond tanned man in the tank top and biker shorts emerged first. He took one look at me and the redhead together and rolled his eyes in derision. "Breeder," he muttered.

A moment later Fister emerged. His shirt was untucked. He accorded the blond man a curt nod. "Thanks, Ted," he said.

Ted returned the nod in kind. "My pleasure,"

he said. And he turned and nodded politely to the woman and to me. "Afternoon," he said, and sauntered off, picking his spandex biker shorts out of his crack.

I shot Fister a glare. "You took your time," I said.

He looked from the woman to me and back to the woman again. "I see you've met my associate," he said to her.

Associate? Even though I still had a pissed woman waving a knife in my general direction, I had enough self-respect to bristle at the designation.

"Identify yourself," the woman said.

"Very well." Fister took a deep breath. "In darkest hour, let all pussy-assed motherfuckers of the nether realms fear our might."

The woman appeared satisfied. She lowered the knife to her side. "For united we stand . . ." she said.

"And liberty and justice for all," Fister concluded.

The woman gave Fister a bow of greeting. "Who are you?" she asked.

"Proctomom3587," Fister said. "And you would be?"

"Gynowench69."

"Ah. So nice to actually make your acquaintance in person, Gynowench. You look nothing like your avatar."

The woman sized Fister up, and subtly licked her lips. "Neither do you."

"I take it you two have met online?" I cut in.

Both Fister and the woman nodded.

"Demonasswhuppers.com."

"Oh. Of course." I looked to the woman. "I hope now that you've both established your bona fides that you can put that knife away before someone gets hurt."

The woman shrugged. She did as I asked, at least: she slid the knife into an ankle sheath obscured by her hooker heels. As she was doing this, I took a few steps closer to Fister and fixed him with a glare. "Demonasswhuppers dot com?"

He shrugged. "Demonfuckeruppers dot com was already taken."

"Oh. Of course. That's the dumbest code phrase I've ever heard, by the way."

Fister shrugged again. "What can I say? I was a little high when I came up with it."

I looked to Gynowench69. "Well . . . do you have a real name?"

"Victoria," she said.

"Nice to meet you, Victoria," I said. "Properly, I mean. Without a knife at my throat."

"Sorry about that," she said. "I had to be sure you weren't working for the enemy."

"Perfectly logical. Anybody could have made the same mistake." I was reaching a little far up my ass for something to say, something to defuse the tension of our meeting. I rocked a little unsteadily on my feet. "So . . . I take it you're a gynecologist?"

She stared at me. "How do you know that?"

"Your screen name. Gynowench69."

"Oh. Yeah. And you? Are you a proctologist, too?"

"Yup. Guilty as charged." I smiled my most disarming smile, pleased we were all getting along at last.

She raised an eyebrow at me. "Long day at the orifice already, eh?"

"Ha ha," I said. "Haven't heard that one before."

She ignored me and addressed herself to Fister. "We've got a problem. Can we go somewhere we can talk?"

Fister considered. "There's a Starbuck's just around the corner—"

"No!" I cut in. "Not Starbucks. Not again."

"All right then. How about Burger King? It's just down the block."

Victoria and I received our Whoppers and took seats a respectable distance from the play area, where a plurality of young mothers pushed strollers and supervised their toddlers or pre-school aged children on the colorful playground equipment: the slide, the tromping bridge, and the spring-mounted teetery thingies in the shapes of animals. I had a few moments alone with her while Fister waited up at the counter as a new batch of French fries finished their deep-greasing. She really was very beautiful, I was free to notice, especially now that she wasn't threatening to kill me any longer.

"So," I said, and cleared my throat. "How long have you been hunting demons?" And immediately thereafter I mentally kicked myself; it was a stupid conversation opener.

But if she thought it odd or even slightly inappropriate, she didn't show it. "About four years," she said. "You?"

"Mmmh." I looked at my watch. "About two hours. Give or take a few minutes."

This earned me a raised eyebrow. "Two hours? Wow. Talk about baptism by fire."

"Quite literally, in this case," I said.

She snorted—a clipped half-chuckle that was perhaps the closest she came to true mirth given her all-business attitude.

She took a bite of her Whopper and looked past me. She'd sat with her back up against one wall of the restaurant, where she had a good view of the entire dining area. I realized she must be scoping out the place . . . looking for menace in every shadow, possible avenues of escape, that sort of thing. All James Bond-y, in a bombshell redhead kind of way.

"So . . ." I tried again to jump-start a conversation. "What's it like? The demon fighting life?"

"It's . . . messy."

"'Messy?'"

"Yeah." She sipped at her Diet Coke, leaving a rouged lipstick stain on the straw. "You know. Demons' easiest point of entry into our realm is through the humors."

"The humors? You mean—"

She held up a hand to cut me off. "I know, I know. It's not sound medicine, it's just a term we in the business have taken to using to refer to demons' likely points of entry into this realm."

"Huh? I don't understand."

She sighed, like she was dealing with a particularly dim student. "Tell me this, then. Why did you decide to become a proctologist?"

"My dad was a proctologist."

"And poking around in assholes runs in the family? I doubt it."

"I—well . . . it's a necessary and vital field of medicine—"

"Don't talk to me like a clinician. Come on. Talk dirty to me."

"What?" I choked a little on my gulp of soda.

She grinned. "Gotcha. Seriously, though. What is it about staring up buttholes that gets you off?"

"It doesn't get me off," I protested. "It's just—"

"Just what?"

I floundered for a moment. I couldn't quite come up with an answer. "Well," I finally countered, hating the prissy sound of my own voice, like I was a ten-year-old who'd just lost a rousing round of *I-know-you-are-but-what-am-I?* "What about you? Why'd you become a gynecologist? Do you like staring up twats all day? You're not a—"

"Lesbian?" she finished for me. "No. But it's all related, you know. It's . . . primal."

"Primal?"

"Of course. Demons, in their purest form, are comprised of the psychic effluvia of human consciousness. To manifest in physical form on our plane of existence, they're drawn to the physical waste of the human body. Ergo . . . it's messy."

"Oh. I see what you mean."

Fister joined us then. He laid his tray loaded with a double Whopper and an extra large order of fries and a giant drum of soda on the table. He looked to Victoria, then to me, and grinned. "Well, you two kids seem to be getting along," he said.

Victoria fixed him with an icy stare. "You know we shouldn't all be here together," she said.

Fister shrugged.

"Wait a second," I cut in. "Why shouldn't we all be here together?"

"Because three of us together is too inviting of a target," Fister said. "Our strict policy . . . we only collaborate online through screen names and avatars. No one is supposed to know anything about any other members of the order."

"'Order?' You have an actual Order?"

"No," Fister said.

"Yes," Victoria said.

Fister shot a look of disgust across the table at Victoria. "Good going. Now he's going to want to join. He's been a sucker for secret societies ever since we were kids. He actually made it all the way through *The Davinci Code*."

Victoria ignored him. "We may need to set aside our policies and pool our resources, just this once." She looked to Fister, then to me. "Something big's coming."

I frowned. "What kind of something?"

"Some sort of über-demon lord. The minor demons and their terrestrial minions have been coordinating their efforts to summon him. The last three exorcisms I performed, all three demons threatened the arrival of their 'master.'"

I shuddered. The words of the demon Fister's and I'd just vanquished only a few hours ago came back to haunt me: *My master will come, and he will have his revenge on you! He will have his revenge on all of humanity!*

"Yeah," Fister admitted, "ours, too."

Victoria sighed. "It's worse than I thought, then."

Fister shrugged. "So tell us what you know."

Victoria spread her hands in a gesture of helplessness. "Nothing. I don't know where or when or even how this demon lord is supposed to cross over."

"A crossing of that magnitude couldn't be done subtly," Fister mused. "That sort of thing would cause one hell of a disturbance in the Force." As soon as the words were out of his mouth he looked to me and held up a hand to forestall any comments. "Don't nerd out on me, that's just a figure of speech."

I scowled at him, but didn't interrupt him.

"We need to talk to Morpheus," Fister concluded.

"Who's Morpheus?" I asked.

"He's the webmaster of demonasswhuppers dot com. "He's . . . badass."

"Oh really? How so?"

"He's scored more demon kills than all of the rest of the Order put together. He founded the website."

"Nobody's heard from Morpheus for the last two weeks," Victoria pointed out. "Either he's gone dark, or . . ." She trailed off.

"Or he's dead," Fister finished for her.

Victoria was silent for a moment as she took another sip of her soda. She brought the lidded plastic cup to her lips . . . and held it there, but didn't sip. Her gaze was suddenly distracted by something over my shoulder. I turned around in my seat to look. "What is it?" I asked.

"You see that woman there?"

I swiveled a half-turn in my chair to see whom she was referring to. As far as I could tell, she was referring to an ordinary-looking woman dressed in jeans and a T-shirt who was heading toward the bathroom at the back of the Burger King. "What about her?" I said.

"She's on the rag."

I frowned. "How can you tell?"

"She's a gynecologist," Fister cut in. "She knows everything there is to know about cun—"

Victoria withered him to silence with a glare. Then, she turned back to me. "The way she walks. She's packing a tampon. I can tell."

"Okay," I said, "so what?"

"So the last three women who went into that bathroom were also on the rag. That can't be a coincidence."

"Then what is it?" I asked. But she left my question unanswered. She stood up and strode with purpose across the restaurant, dodging a young father bearing a loaded tray of Parfaits toward the booth in the corner. I paused just long enough to shoot Fister a puzzled look. He responded by shrugging, then he, too, stood to follow Victoria across the restaurant.

Victoria stalked down the restaurant's back hallway with Fister and me in close pursuit. When she reached the women's restroom, she kicked open the door with no warning whatsoever to whoever was inside.

I came to stand behind her, and the scene inside the women's restroom caused my blood to chill in my veins. Three young women lay on the floor, unconscious—or dead; I couldn't tell which. Their legs were splayed wide open, with dark red stains covering their clothing.

A fourth woman was on her feet with some infernal miniature Alien-looking creature with its jaws clamped onto her cooze. The woman seemed utterly oblivious: she merely stared straight ahead into the bathroom mirror, her expression one of blissful abstraction. As I stared, utterly dumbfucked, the creature's body, which was about the size of a six-month old baby, seemed to pulsate once . . . and grow.

And then, as if it had sucked all the nourishment it could out of the woman's hoo-hah, the creature released its hold and dropped down onto the floor. It looked up at Victoria and hissed, displaying rows of razor-sharp feral teeth.

Victoria whipped out a pistol from some holster I didn't even know she had and trained it on the creature. But before she could fire off a shot, the creature burst into motion. It skittered through Victoria's legs, arced around Fister and me, and sped out of the restaurant through the half-open glass door, past a stunned-looking older gentleman who could only watch it speed away as if his old eyes were deceiving him.

The woman's stupor broke.   She sighed daintily, and sank to the bathroom floor.   Victoria took only one step forward into the women's bathroom and caught her by the shoulders.   She eased the woman down onto the restroom's tiled floor.

The woman smiled beatifically and slowly swiveled her head to look at Victoria. "Did you see her?" she said. "She's beautiful, isn't she?"

"Where is it going?" Victoria asked the woman. And when she got no immediate response, she shook the woman by the shoulders. *"Where?"*

"To school," the woman replied, and giggled.

"School? What school?"

"Oh, you know where."   The woman smiled broadly, an eerie reflection of the jaw-baring hiss the creature had just given us. "She's going after your son."

CHAPTER THREE

Victoria blinked once, twice at the woman on the bathroom floor. Then, she whirled around, sprinted past Fister and me, causing the both of us to dive against the wall of the back hallway that led to the Burger King's customer restrooms lest she bodily shove us out of the way. Then, she disappeared out the side entrance of the restaurant.

A second later, Fister followed suit. Which meant that I was the slowest on the draw. I wrestled with indecision: should I follow them? There were four bleeding women on the floor, and I was a doctor, after all . . .

Ultimately, I did what any sane man would do when confronted with four women bleeding out their twats: I ran. I at least paused for one second at the restaurant's exit and shouted, "Call 911!" Then I booked it after Fister.

When I made it out into the parking lot, Victoria was already in the driver's seat of her Azera with the engine started. Fister had the passenger side door open and was climbing in. I estimated I had somewhere between one and two seconds before Victoria got the vehicle in gear and pealed out of the parking lot. So I sprinted across the narrow parking lot and reached for the handle to the back seat. Just as I arrived, Victoria confirmed my expectations and whipped the car into reverse. I lost my grip on the handle. I stumbled backward just quickly enough to avoid having my feet crunched under Victoria's tires.

I stared balefully at the vehicle. At any moment Victoria would peal out of the parking lot, leaving me in the dust. But my salvation came in the form of a navy blue Prius that came out of the drive-thru lane and pulled in front of Victoria, cutting off her exit onto the road. She laid on the horn.

Fister took advantage of the moment's delay to open his passenger side door. "Get in!" He beckoned to me.

I did as he bid. I sprinted a few paces to catch up to the car, and just as Victoria decided not to wait on the car blocking her way in front of her and whip her Azera around to the side and off the curb, I dove ass-over-teakettle into the passenger seat.

Right into Fister's lap. He yelped as I unwittingly mashed his nards trying to gain position. At the same time Victoria stepped on the accelerator. My torso was firmly in the passenger seat draped over Fister's lap, but my ass and my legs were still dangling precariously out the open passenger side door.

Right then, the car jounced like a motherfuck as Victoria launched it off the curb and onto the street. If it hadn't been for Fister clutching my ass,

I'd have fallen backward onto the street. Fortunately, once the jarring from our plunge off the curb was complete, Fister managed to keep his grip on my ass with one hand and grope around my knees with his other hand. He tipped me into the car. My face came close enough to deep throat Victoria's gear shift at the car's floor while my feet thudded against the passenger mirror, nearly knocking it off its hinge.

After a good bit of shuffling and indecorous clutching, Fister and I managed to get me right-way-round enough so that Fister could reach out and heave closed the passenger side door.

I came to rest sitting in Fister's lap, uncomfortably far forward toward the dashboard of the car.

"Nice of you to join us," Victoria muttered to me as she flew down the street well in excess of the speed limit.

Fister managed to extricate his left arm from where it was mashed between my back and his chest. He did the only thing he could do: he wrapped it around my chest in a cramped bear hug. "Ooh, Mikey," he said in my ear, and if I'd been facing him I'm sure he would have been flashing me his adolescent grin. "I hate to tell you this, but you're giving me a boner."

I took a huge breath, both to try to catch my breath after my ordeal and also to keep myself from hyperventilating at Victoria's craptacularly unsafe driving. As I was clutched rather indecorously on Fister's lap, unstrapped in, all it would take was one false move on Victoria's part and I'd be squirted through the windshield in turbo mode.

"What the hell was that thing?" I asked.

Fister answered: "Cunilingual demon. Feeds on menstrual ejecta."

"I gathered that much. Is it susceptible to Catholic iconography, too, or is it banished with a liberal dose of Midol?"

Victoria answered. "Nah. We'll take this little bitch out the old-fashioned way." With the hand that wasn't grasping the steering wheel, she stroked the butt of the pistol that was resting in her lap.

"You can't go firing a weapon in an LA public school," I pointed out.

"You think they'll think I'm a student?"

"Ha ha. Not likely, but you'll have SWAT teams crawling all over the school. They'll shoot you first and ask questions never."

"This is my son we're talking about. Those fuckers sent a demon after my son. This shit's personal now." Victoria took a left turn without bothering to slow down more than a token amount. The g-forces pressed me even tighter up against Fister and his boner.

"I sympathize, but hot heads sink ships."

"That's loose lips," Fister butted in. "Loose lips sink ships."

"Whatever. I'm just—"

"Reach into the glove box," Victoria instructed me, paying me no attention whatsoever.

"What?"

"Reach into the glove box."

I did as she bid. As close as I was to the glove box, I had to suck in my stomach and press backward against Fister in order to open the lid. But when I managed to get it open, I stared inside and saw why she'd instructed me to do so. Inside, she had one of those magnetic flashing lights that could be fixed to the roof of a vehicle. "Where did you get that?" I asked.

"From a snowplow in Colorado," Victoria answered. "Not police issue at all, but people don't tend to fuck with cars that have flashing lights on the roof. Hand it over."

I did. She took it, flicked a switch on it to turn on the flashing, then opened her window, leaned out a little, and clamped it to the roof of the vehicle above her. The whole maneuver only compromised her driving by a few swerves that came precariously close to occasioning shit-stains in my underwear.

Once with the flashing light atop her car, Victoria was emboldened to drive even faster, so she floored it and raced down the road, swerving in and out of vehicles that were suddenly driving very, very carefully indeed. The only time LA drivers drive carefully is when they see flashing lights in their rearview mirrors, apparently.

"We need to get those kids out of the school," Victoria said. "Force an evacuation."

"No problem," Fister said. "We pull the fire alarm."

"I like the way you think, but it's not good enough. A fire alarm will cause an evacuation, and we'll get maybe twenty minutes max until they determine it's a false alarm. Kids pull the fire alarm all the time." She considered. After a second, her face brightened. "We need a bomb threat!"

"A *what*?" I said. "You can't seriously call in a bomb threat to a public school. That's gotta be like a federal offense or something."

"Do the math," Victoria told me. "In a middle school of two thousand students, how many girls do you think are likely to be on the rag at any given moment?"

I actually did the math in my head. "Maybe about a hundred, give or take," I said.

"Exactly. That's a hundred prime targets for a pudenda carnidactalis."

"A what?"

"Snatch-eating demon," Fister translated for me.

"Not to mention anybody else that just happens to get in the way of its teeth. I'm not liking the potential body count scenario. We need to remove all the potential targets from its path, make sure it stays small. To do that, we need to make sure the school is evacuated. It won't attack huge crowds, not while it's still in its infancy. We need a bomb threat."

"I'm on it," Fister said. He stuck his hand in my pants pocket as he fished for my cell phone.

"Hey!" I squeaked. "Watch the—"

"Mikey, behave!" Fister admonished. He grasped my cell phone and, given the complexities of our seating arrangement, struggled to hold it so he could dial.

"You can't use my cell phone to call in a bomb threat," I protested. "They'll have caller ID—"

"Don't worry," Fister said. "I've got it all taken care of. Think of the lives you're saving, Mikey." He thumbed on the voice features of my iphone and told Siri to look up the number for— "Wait, what school?" he asked Victoria.

"Holmes."

When he got the number from Siri, he instructed her to dial. He waited for a few seconds for the phone to ring, and when somebody picked up, he said, "There's a bomb in your school. It's going to go off in twenty minutes." And then, as if to make himself sound more convincing, he followed up with a maniacal chuckle. Then he hung up.

"Great," I muttered. "Just what I wanted . . . a visit by the police."

"Don't worry," Fister said. He hit the switch to roll down the window and chucked my iphone out the window.

"Hey!" I cried. "That's brand new!"

"You can report it stolen," Fister said. "Whoever picks it up and tries to pawn it'll get fingered for calling in a bomb threat. Serves 'em right, don't you think?"

I thought it was small recompense for losing my iphone, but I could only sulk in silence.

After another seven minutes of swerving, lane-switching, birdie-flipping, and near-death experiences, Victoria screeched the Azera to a halt on a side street overlooking Holmes Middle School. Hundreds and hundreds of teenagers loitered around outside on the football field as a result of the bomb scare, chaperoned by teachers and staff members. It looked surprisingly orderly given the sheer number of teenagers involved. I was relieved that the sacrifice of my iphone had not been in vain; Fister's bomb threat had done the trick and gotten the building evacuated.

Victoria hopped out of her vehicle without even bothering to close her door and started scanning the crowd of teenagers. "*Goddammit!*" she swore a moment later. "I can't see him."

"What does he look like?" Fister asked.

"You can't miss him. He looks like a beaver."

"A beaver?"

"Like mother, like son," Fister muttered.

"Something like that." Victoria waved a hand dismissively. "He told me about it once."

I wondered fleetingly what the hell a middle schooler who looked like a beaver was supposed to look like. I scanned the football field of adolescents along with Fister and Victoria. Nothing.

"He's not here," Victoria said. "Dammit, where is he?"

She burst into motion, heading along the fence that ringed our end of the football field toward the school. She set a stiff pace for Fister and me to follow, and while she walked she fished her cell phone out of her pocket and fiddled with the keypad to dial. She held the phone to her ear and waited while it rang. At length she hung up and swore. "That boy," she said. "Must have gotten his phone taken away by his history teacher again."

Victoria's trajectory took us around the back corner of the school, and cut us off from view of the football field and all the students on it. From what I could tell, this seemed to be an auxiliary wing of the school—maybe for shop classes or industrial arts or something. There was a set of double glass doors on this wing of the school. Victoria strode up to them and tried the door. Locked.

"Are you sure about this?" I asked, looking in both directions to see if anyone were in sight. Breaking into a school during an active bomb threat had to be an even lousier idea than Perestroika. "How do you know your son's even inside?"

"Because the demon's inside, and that bitch back at the Burger King conjured the demon specifically to go after my son. To fuck with me."

I frowned. "How can you know the demon's inside the school?"

"Because there's only one side of this building that's not visible from a road, and the demon had the same idea we did." She pointed to the ground at our feet. I looked down and saw little specks of blood leading in a trail across the threshold of the door and into the school.

Victoria swore. "Except it must have had a student to let it in."

"Nice trick," Fister said. "Hypnotizing women on the rag. If I could just bottle that and sell it—"

Victoria strode a few paces past the double doors and stopped at a classroom window. She stood on tiptoes and jiggled the window open. Then, she turned to Fister. "Give me a lift," she instructed.

Fister looked like he'd won the lottery, with an

open invitation to stare up her skirt. He hastened to lace his fingers together to give her a hoist up. She stepped into his grip and he hoisted her up onto the window ledge. It took her a second to crawl inside, and in the time it took her to do so, Fister drank an eyeful of her black lace thong panties. I'd like to say I took the high road and looked away, but . . . well . . .

Once she was through, Fister turned to me. "I think I just found religion." He grinned.

I shook my head. "Ted would be jealous," I said.

He frowned. "Ted? Who's Ted?"

"Never mind. Come on." I laced my fingers together and nodded to him to climb in after Victoria.

He held up a hand to turn down my offer of assistance. "Oh, no, thank you," he said. "Remember, I threw my back out a couple of weeks ago doing gymnastics."

"You've never done a day of gymnastics in your life."

"No, but I did a gymnast. It's practically the same thing."

"You mean you're just going to let her go in there alone to face a bloody twat-demon all by herself? What kind of a demon hunter are you?"

"The kind who'll wait for her to open the door for me." He cocked his chin to indicate that I should look over my shoulder. I turned, and saw that Victoria was standing a few paces off holding open the set of double doors. Fister trotted past me and entered the school. "Thanks," he said to

Victoria.

I hesitated there for a second. Victoria was waiting at the door for me to follow Fister. I felt a sudden stab of terror. My brilliant plan of hoisting Fister into the classroom and then standing watch outside here evaporated in a puff of smoke. "I—" I couldn't think of a likely excuse to remain outside the building, so I dutifully trotted over and entered the building.

Once inside, Victoria took the lead. She proceeded, bent over low to the ground to follow the trail of bloodstains on the tiled floors. It was a ridiculously easy trail to follow.

Not surprisingly, the trail of blood made an immediate detour into the first girls' restroom we passed. "Fuck," Victoria muttered.

My heart missed a beat when I thought about all the used tampons that might be in the tampon disposal in a girls' restroom in a school this size. For this demon, they had to be like delicious little pouches of Red Bull. For all I knew, this much of a pre-menstrual bacchanal might have literally given the demon wings.

The trail of blood continued on down the hall. Apparently, after the demon had exhausted its supply of delicious treats, it had reemerged. We passed several classrooms on the industrial arts wing and turned a corner into what appeared to be a foreign language wing, judging by the predominance of posters of Garfield and *Twilight* characters with speech bubbles saying things in foreign languages. Here, the trail of blood stopped.

"GodmotherfuckingJesusHChristdammit!"
Victoria swore.

I frowned. "What—I don't understand," I said.
"How could it just stop?"

"It's smart," Victoria answered. "It knew we'd
follow it. It left a false trail for us."

"But then . . . is it even inside the school?"

"Oh, it's here," Victoria said. "But it could be
anywhere in the school." She looked up and down
the hall, and the expression of pure, vulnerable
helplessness on her face nearly broke my heart.
"*Henry!*" she called out. "*Henry*, can you hear
me?"

Fister lunged at her and clamped his hand over
her mouth. "Don't," he said. "You don't need to
let the demon know exactly where we are. We're
supposed to be hunting it, not the other way
around."

I had to agree with Fister. Much as I
sympathized with Victoria's concern for her son, I
thought broadcasting our location to any denizen of
hell within earshot was a supremely bad idea.

We froze like that for a long moment: me
fretting my ass to smithereens, Fister with his hand
clamped over Victoria's mouth. And the echoing
silence of the abandoned school mocked us.

But then Fister cocked his head to the side and
scrunched up his lips. "Do you hear that?" he said.

I listened. At first I heard nothing, but then, a
moment later, I heard what Fister had heard. It was
coming from somewhere across the school, barely
within earshot. It was a high-pitched demonic
screeching sound, no less blood-curdling for being

barely audible.

Victoria bolted. She broke free of Fister's grip and headed directly in the direction of the sound. I thought that that was most likely a terrible idea as well, but it's not like anybody solicited my input or anything. Fister tore off hot on her heels, once again leaving me there wrestling with my own internal sense of prudence. I could either rush headlong toward a demon with giant blood-dripping fangs, or I could make a break in the opposite direction.

"Damn you, Fister," I muttered to myself. And I hotfooted it after him and Victoria.

The screeching sound grew louder as we bolted down a corridor, then turned a corner and continued down another. Though as we neared, I realized the screeching sound was now muffled somehow, as if—

—as if it was stuck inside a locker. We skidded to a halt at the foot of a stairwell adjacent to a row of lockers. The screeching, like the keening wail of a banshee, was coming from inside the third locker. It was punctuated by echoing thuds from the inside that visibly dented the red-painted metal of the locker.

The three of us stood there, staring gape-mouthed at our good fortune. And as we watched, the door of the locker directly next to the one where the demon was trapped swung open, and a boy in a furry costume stepped out. His expression was somewhat self-satisfied . . .

"Henry!"

But it morphed into confusion at the sound of

Victoria's voice.   He turned to stare at Victoria.
"Mom?" he said, incredulous.

Victoria dashed across the distance separating
them.   But the boy held out a hand to stop her
before she could wrap him in an instinctive
embrace.   "Hold on a second," he said.   He
gestured to the locker containing the demon.   "I've
kind of got a . . . thing."

He produced a can of Right Guard aerosol
from a deep pocket on his striped furry costume,
then followed it with a lighter.   He strode up to the
locker.   Then, he flicked the lighter, and held the tip
of the aerosol can to the flame and sprayed a plume
of fire into the top vent of the locker.   Then, he
repeated the maneuver at the locker's bottom vent.

The result was instantaneous.   The screeching
of the demon inside the locker transmogrified into a
high-pitched shriek of pain.   Whatever was inside
the locker must have served as effective kindling,
because flickering tongues of flame belched out of
the locker's vents on the top and the bottom.

After a long last piteous wail of agony tapered
off into silence, Victoria's stalled reunion with her
son jump-started again.   She clutched her furry-clad
son in her arms in a fierce bear hug and sobbed out
her relief into his neck.   "I was so worried," she
said.

The boy shrugged her away.   "Mom!" he said,
and the vowel came out sounding like two
syllables: *mah-ahm.*   "I'm fine."   He beamed up at
her.   Then, he blinked at Fister and me.   "Who are
they?" he asked.

Victoria waved a hand at us dismissively.   "Oh.

They're just some proctologists I found in the park."

The boy frowned. "What's a proctologist?" he asked.

Victoria didn't seem too apt to reply anytime soon, so I piped up: "We're specialists in rectal medicine—"

"Oh," the boy said. "Asshole doctors. I see."

Since we'd been officially introduced, Fister and I drew closer. I examined the boy's handiwork with the locker, which was now pouring out a blackish smoke with an utterly noxious odor. Any moment now it was sure to set off the fire alarm.

"Nice work," I said.

"Thanks." He beamed. "It took a semester's worth of Spanish homework to serve as kindling."

"How'd you get it to go into the locker?"

The boy shrugged. "I stole all the tampons from all three bathrooms on second floor and dumped em in there. It's Mason Granger's locker. He's a real douchebag."

"Nice," I said. "How'd you know it'd go after tampons?"

The boy scowled. "What, you've never seen a vag demon before?"

"I—well . . . not exactly."

"Christ. Amateurs."

Victoria fixed the boy with an admonishing glare that carried absolutely no heat. Odd. When I'd met her at the park, with her knife at my throat, she'd been able to glare holes into my soul as naturally as blinking. But with her son, she seemed as stern as a doting grandparent. "Henry, have you been snooping in my internet history again?" she said. "I've told you a hundred times—"

Henry rolled his eyes in the universal teenage expression of *yeah yeah, yadda yadda.* He ignored her and stepped over to address himself to Fister and to me. "Her porn's pretty kinky, too," he said as an aside to us. "I'm Henry," he said. He reached out his hand to shake Fister's hand, then mine.

"Nice to meet you, Henry," I said. I sized up his furry costume. "So you're a . . . um . . ."

"A honey badger," he said.

I shook my head, nonplussed.

"A nasty ass honey badger?" He prompted.

Still I shook my head.

"You know? Because I don't give a fuck."

I could only stare at him, now utterly confused.

He rolled his eyes again. He turned back to his mother. "Where do you find them?" he muttered.

"We'd better get out of here," Fister said. "I think the fire alarm's going to go off any second."

"You're probably right," Victoria said. She spoke to her son. "Come on. I'm parked out back. I don't think you'll have any more classes today anyway."

"Yeah, that was awesome," Henry said. "They announced a bomb threat right as I realized there was a vag demon in the building. Was that you?"

"It was him, actually." Victoria pointed to me. "What did you say your name was again, anyway?"

I didn't answer her. I was looking at the still smoking locker.

Fister and Victoria looked at me. "Mikey,

what is it?" Fister asked.

I looked to Henry. "You said you emptied out all the tampon disposals from the girls' bathrooms on the second floor?" I said.

"Yeah."

I looked to Victoria and Fister. "But this is the first floor, right?"

"Yeah?" Victoria said. "So?"

"We saw the demon's trail go into a girls' bathroom here on this floor. If it snacked on a handful of tampons in there . . ."

"What are you getting at, Mikey?" Fister asked, impatient.

I tried to reconcile my mental recollection of the demon from the Burger King, and how it had grown in contact with menstrual blood. "Then it should be too big to fit in that locker," I concluded.

I hate it when I'm right. At that moment a preternatural roar bellowed out from the top of the stairs. I yanked my gaze to focus on the top of the stairs. There, another of the twat demon monstrosities, bathed in oozing red blood, loomed on the landing. And this one was big—easily a head taller than Fister or me. It opened its mouth and hissed in anger, baring its blood-dripping fangs.

"Fuck!" Henry swore. "Twins!"

I backed up a step. While we'd been chatting away here, this one must have been sucking all the tampons dry on the upper floor of the school. "Got any more brilliant plans?" I asked Henry.

"Um . . . run, maybe?" Henry said.

Sounded like a prime idea to me. Henry

bolted.   I followed suit, following the puffy wagging tail on his honey badger outfit. Fister and Victoria dogged my heels. The creature bellowed a queefing, snorting sound of rage behind us and lumbered after.

Henry led us down a corridor into what I assumed was the science wing. There, he chose the second to last classroom on the wing before the corridor dead-ended. We all piled in after him and slammed the door closed. I fumbled with the door, looking around for a locking mechanism, but found nothing.

"Help me!" Fister called. He started moving some of the student desks to block the door.

"Mom, you help him," Henry instructed. "You." Henry pointed to me. "Give me a hand."

I followed him. I suffered a brief flash of cognitive dissonance as I realized I was following the orders of a thirteen year-old kid, but it dissipated quickly as the demon twat monster thudded against the classroom door.

Henry led me to a closet at the back of the room. He jiggled the handle, but it was locked. "We need to get in here," Henry said.

"Why?"

Henry fixed me with his withering *what-the-fuck* scowl. "This is the chemistry room. This is where they keep the hydrochloric acid."

"Oh."

"Well go on. Kick it in." Henry pointed at the little bunny slippers on his costume. "I'm not exactly dressed for it."

I did as he instructed. I pulled back and kicked

at the door right above the lock, as scores and scores of detective shows and crime novels I'd read as a kid claimed was the optimal place for kicking in a door.

The door didn't budge.

"Christ," Henry muttered. "Come on, will ya?"

Gritting my teeth, I tried again. Still no give on the door. A half a heartbeat later, the meager thud of my foot's impact on the closet door was echoed by a much more resounding thud from the twat beast outside the classroom door. Fister's and Victoria's hastily erected barrier of student desks slid a few inches from the impact.

I kicked at the door again. It flexed a little this time, but only a little.

"You really oughta spend some time in the gym, you know," Henry said. "Reaching up buttholes all day—"

I didn't let him finish his sentence. I fucking hated it when people insulted protologists. I erupted with a berserker howl and delivered my best kick yet to the stubborn door. This time, it flew open.

Henry raced into the closet just as the twat demon outside managed to overcome Fister's and Victoria's flimsy defenses and piledriver into the classroom, spraying student desks in all directions. It paused to howl its rage as it stepped across the threshold into the classroom.

"Here." Henry emerged from the closet and passed me a bottle marked "HCl." "Lock and load," he said. And, not waiting for me, he chucked a bottle of his own at the creature.

I copied his example. It was the best weapon we had against the creature, even though a little niggling fear at the back of my mind fretted that whatever kind of middle-school grade hydrochloric acid they were storing in this chemicals closet would have barely more acidic potency than lemonade.

Henry's throw and mine both scored direct hits. Our flasks of acid both smashed to shards against the creature's hide and sloshed acid all over. Despite my fears, it appeared as if the contents of the flasks was potent enough to at least piss the creature off. It hunkered back a little under the impact and roared in fury.

"It's working!" Henry said. He ducked back inside the closet and emerged again a second later with more bottles of chemicals. "Fire at will."

I needed no encouragement. The contents of the closet were the only weapon we had against the creature. I chucked another flask at the terrible creature. This one failed to hit the creature directly, but it smashed into tiny fragments against the wall beside the door, and the liquid contents of the flask sprayed out all over its face and into its eyes.

Henry and I kept up our barrage, not giving the creature enough time to react between bombardments. It recoiled, trying in vain to back out into the hallway, but Henry and I followed it out there and continued pelting it. In short order we had it curled into a ball on the ground.

I chucked one last vial after it, and then Henry closed in for the kill. He drew nearer to the creature, fished out his aerosol can of deodorant from a pocket of his honey badger outfit, then flicked on his lighter, and sprayed directly at the creature's eyes. The creature, doused in hydrochloric acid and whatever else we'd thrown at it, lit up like a piece of charcoal doused with premium lighter fluid.

"Um—that's not a good—" I began.

Thankfully, Victoria swooped in. She dashed into the hall, picked up her son, and hauled him bodily back into the classroom   —

"—idea."

—just as the creature exploded in a spray of menstrual ejecta. Fister shielded his eyes. Victoria shielded her son with her body, and the red rain of ick splattered all over their backs, staining their clothes and their hair.

The threat was removed. All that remained of the creature was a misshapen lump of flesh in the middle of the hallway outside the classroom that was still lit by tiny flickering flames that were rapidly dying out.

Slowly, Victoria released her son from her grasp. She, Henry, Fister and I came to stand over the carcass of the creature. "Yeah, motherfucker!" Henry cheered. And given the circumstance, I understood completely that his mother didn't chastise him for his use of language.

"Now what?" I asked. "Do we just—?"

"Mom," Henry said, "look away."

Victoria frowned. "What? I don't—"

"Just look away. Please."

Puzzled, she did as her son bid. Henry reached

down and unzipped the fly of his honey badger costume. He rummaged around inside the crotch for a second, and then extricated his pecker. Then, he urinated on the carcass of the twat demon.

I frowned. "What's that for?" I asked. "Is it to—?"

Henry smiled. "It's my signature move. I always pee on the demons I kill. It's like spiking the football." His stream was strong, and it made a satisfying *pitter*ing sound on the demon's carcass.

Fister stared at the kid, realization dawning. "Morpheus?" he said.

Henry smiled. "Nice to meet you—um—?"

"Proctomom69."

"I see. Well, at least you don't seem quite as gay as your screen name." Henry nodded at the creature's corpse as his stream piddled out. He jiggled a few times, and then tucked himself back in. "Give it a go if you like."

Fister needed little encouragement. He unzipped and let fly, chortling like a retarded third grader in the process.

"Um, are you boys finished yet?" Victoria piped up, still shielding her eyes.

"Yeah," Henry said, even though Fister was still midstream.

Victoria unshielded her eyes. She looked at Fister's midsection, and apparently finding nothing of interest there, she focused her gaze instead on her son. "Morpheus?" she said. "You're . . . you're Morpheus?"

Henry looked like a little boy who'd just been caught masturbating. "Yeah," he said in a small voice.

A long silence stretched between them. An entire range of emotions flickered across Victoria's face in the space of only a few seconds. Finally, she found her voice. "You are in so much trouble when we get home, mister."

CHAPTER FOUR

After some of the shell-shock from the morning's events wore off, we piled in Victoria's Azera while we decided where to go. This time, at least, I was able to climb into the back seat on the passenger side, with Henry occupying the back seat behind his mother.

"We can't go to your place," Fister said to Victoria. "Not right away, at any rate. They've got your scent. They sent two pudenda carnidactialises after Morhpeus here. Which means he's been compromised."

Victoria fixed her son with a glare in the rearview mirror that said louder than words: *You are in such trouble for spearheading a secret society for the extermination of demons without my knowledge, mister.*

"We shouldn't go to my place, either," Fister said. "I'm . . . well . . . I'm . . ."

"You're an utterly fearsome demon hunter," Victoria finished for him.

"Well, I don't like to brag—"

Victoria pinned me with her eyes in the

rearview mirror. "So it looks like we're going to your place. You're new to the whole game. They shouldn't have fingered you yet."

"I—" I stammered in an attempt to find words, but abandoned the attempt as Henry sniggered at the use of the word "fingered." Demon ass whupper or not, he was still thirteen.

"So where to?"

Reluctantly, I gave Victoria directions on how to drive to my apartment. No one spoke any further for the duration of the ride, but I did notice Victoria, Fister, and Henry alike paying especial attention to the traffic behind us—just in case.

Finally we arrived at my apartment. I turned the key in the door and ushered in my three companions before me. My breath caught in my throat a little as I stepped across the threshold after them: I'd just been present and done my (albeit) small part in helping to rid the world of not one, not two, but three demons this morning. Would the denizens of the netherworld and their earthly minions have fingered me as well? Were my relative days of safely whiling away the evenings over a book of Sudoku and a little tug to orgy porn be numbered?

"Whoa," Henry breathed when he saw my condo. "Nice. This is a killer poon pad." Which I took to mean, in thirteen-year-old lingo, that it was clean and relatively spacious.

Fister chuckled at Henry's enthusiasm. "Except the only poon this place has seen in the last two years is—"

"Can I get you guys anything to drink?" I cut

him off before he could spill all the secrets of my meager love life over the last two years. I glanced nervously at Victoria and smiled, and when she met my gaze I surreptitiously looked away.

I poured a glass of Chardonnay for Victoria, a scotch for Fister from my liquor cabinet, and poured out the last of a two-liter of Diet Pepsi for Henry. Then, I fixed myself a martini. It was only three o'clock in the afternoon, but dammit, I'd deserved it today.

"So now what?" Victoria said as we all sat around my living room sipping our drinks.

"Something big's coming," Fister said. "They wouldn't have tried to take out Morpheus—sorry, I mean Henry—if they weren't afraid of what he'd do."

Henry spread his hands helplessly. "Sorry. I'm afraid I'm not up on the latest. I've been off the grid for the past two weeks." He glared at his mother. "Somebody took away my laptop for that stupid D minus in Social Studies."

His mother returned his glare. "You never bothered to tell me you were Morpheus," she returned.

"You'd just have flipped out."

"You're damned right—"

"Ahm, maybe we could focus on the matter at hand," I cut in. "So there's some big demon that's getting ready to cross over into our world, I gather? How exactly does that happen?"

"Well," Henry took a sip of his soda, grimaced—either because it was flat, or because it was diet, or both—then said, "generally, most demons that cross over into our world are pussies. To get any of the elder demon lords in any sort of physical incarnation onto the Earthly plane takes a coordinated effort from a whole bunch of worshippers."

"I see," I said. "And just how is it you know all this?"

Henry shrugged. "Wikipedia."

"Ah. So just how many demon worshippers are we talking about, then?"

"Depends upon how big and how bad the demon they're attempting to incarnate is. I'm guessing anywhere from twenty to a hundred."

"I see. So we need to look for a large congregation of demon worshippers, then."

"Well, theoretically. Only it's not usually that easy."

"Of course not," I said. *Why would it be*? Already I was beginning to cultivate a distinct dislike for this demon hunting schtick, because it seemed like we were far more conspicuous than those on the opposite side.

"It's not like people print up business cards that say 'demon worshipper,'" Henry said. "And they don't generally use the internet."

"I see. So can't we just turn this over to the police or something? I mean, leave an anonymous tip, maybe? We don't have to tell the police they're demon conjurers . . . we can just say we suspect them of cooking meth or something."

Henry shook his head. "The police don't have any kind of preparation to deal with elder demon lords. If one manages to cross over, the death count would be catastrophic. No. We've got to find these people and stop them before they can incarnate their demon lord."

"All right, then. How do we do that? I would imagine that kind of a badass demon crossing over would create one hell of a disturbance in the Force, or some shit like that."

"Well, yeah, but not one that we can detect. But the demons of the nether realms would know all about it."

"So how do we get one of them to talk to us?" I asked.

"Well," Henry said, "theoretically, we could summon one. Offer one of us to serve as a vessel."

"You mean like the man we helped this morning was just a vessel?" I shuddered, and looked to Fister. "That one hadn't been fully incarnated yet, right?"

"Right," Fister said. "A run-of-the-mill demon possession starts when the demonic spirit gains control of someone's physical body. If left unchecked, then . . ."

"Then what?" I prompted.

"Well, then the demon seed actually takes root in the person's body and grows until the demon can cast off the shell of the body and burst fully into our world."

"Cheery," I said. "I bet that's . . . messy."

"Yeah," Henry said. "But the nice thing is that in the early stages of possession, a demon isn't all that powerful. So you can ask them questions."

I frowned. "I can't imagine they'd really be all that inclined to talk to you."

"They are if you give them what they want," Henry said.

A brief silence hung around the room. Victoria, Fister, and Henry all exchanged knowing looks with each other, and of course, I was the odd one out. "What?" I asked at length. "What is it?"

"Oh no," Victoria said. "Henry, you can't be serious—"

"Why not?" he said. "It's the perfect opportunity. Angraphilic Eritifal demons are pretty low risk, you've gotta admit."

"Yes, but . . . in order to keep it talking . . ."

Henry shrugged. "Yeah. There could be worse things."

"But . . . ew."

"Come on, mom. You admitted yourself that there could be thousands of lives at stake. The demon lord could be summoned at any moment, and then we're all fucked."

"Henry! Language! We're guests."

Henry scowled. He looked to me. "Sorry," he mumbled. "But we would be totally poked up the ass with a sawed-off broomstick."

"Poetic," I said, holding up a hand to forestall any further euphemisms. "I get the message." I looked to Fister, then to Victoria. "Are you all seriously suggesting one of us volunteer to be the vessel for a demon from the netherworld? I mean, what could possibly go wrong with that plan?"

Fister spread his hands helplessly. "Time is of the essence."

I looked to all three of them. They all seemed to be in agreement. "You've done this before, I take it?" I asked.

"Fuck, no," Henry said. "But don't worry. I can do it."

"Let me guess. Wikipedia?"

Henry nodded.

"That's . . . reassuring."

"All right then," I said, sighing. "Which one of us gets to be the vessel?"

Henry considered. "That depends upon the type of demon we summon. I recommend we contact an Angraphilic Eritifal."

"A what?"

"They're minor demons, in the grand scheme of things. They're really not interested in wreaking mayhem and death and destruction."

"What are they interested in then?" I asked.

"Well . . ." Henry said, "basically, they're just horny."

"Oh. I see."

"So it should be one of us," Fister said, indicating himself, me, and Henry. "All we really need to do to keep one of them talking is keep it . . . stimulated."

I grimaced. "What do you mean by that exactly?"

"A hand job should suffice. Maybe tickle its balls a little bit." Fister looked expectantly at Victoria.

"Uh-uh. No way. I'm not giving anybody a hand job in front of my thirteen year-old son."

"Fine, then," Fister said. "You could be the vessel. Mikey's bound to have a dildo lying around here somewhere."

"Ewww," Henry said. "Please, anything but that. I can't—you can't . . . she's my mother. I'll be the vessel."

"You most certainly will not," Victoria told him. "You're thirteen years old. Demon or no, I'm not letting these gentlemen give you a handjob. That's illegal. In fact, I think you'd better stay in the other room—"

"You can't do this without me," Henry pointed out. "You're a fine demon hunter, mom, but we both know you're shit when it comes to arcane magic."

Victoria sighed. "All right, then. But it's gotta be one of those two." She pointed to Fister and me. "There's no other way."

Henry looked at us expectantly.

My jaw dropped. I looked in horror back and forth between the two of them when I realized what they were suggesting. "I . . . no . . . that's not . . ." I forced myself to stop stammering and summon a coherent sentence. "Fister and I have been friends since grade school."

"So you're perfect, then," Victoria concluded. "You must have already given each other a handjob or two, maybe more, if you grew up together."

"I—how do you know that?"

Victoria rolled her eyes. "Come on. My son's thirteen. I know what he gets up to when he has his little friends over in his room."

"*Mom!*" Henry cried. This time it was a plaintive, two-syllable cry for mercy: *Maaaa-aaahm!*

Fister considered. "Come on, Mikey. It'll be

just like junior high all over again."

I scrunched my eyes closed and shook my head in resignation. "That's . . . so . . . awkward."

"Aw, that's cute," Victoria said. "You're bashful. But come on. What are friends for? Rock paper scissors it out and get it over with."

There was nothing else for it. Resigned, I made a fist, shook it two times, as did Fister, and on the third time, I made the sign of paper.

Fister made scissors.

I'd lost. But I realized with some consternation that I wasn't sure what the consequence of being the loser was. Which was worse: being the vessel, or the . . . what the hell was it? . . . the stroker of the vessel?

I didn't have to wait long to find out. Henry turned to me. "We need to bind him," he said. "For his safety and ours. We need handcuffs."

"I don't just happen to have handcuffs lying around the house," I said.

"Yes, you do," Fister said. "They're in the bottom drawer of the nightstand in your guest bedroom."

"What?" I frowned. "How do you know that? I didn't—"

"You know. When I housesat for you when you went to Cancun a couple of months ago."

I glared at Fister. "And you forgot to take them with you? My mother stayed in the guest bedroom just last month."

Fister shrugged.

We all recused to the guest bedroom. I opened the bottom drawer of the nightstand, and just as

Fister had said, found a sterling pair of handcuffs there, right underneath a copy of a knitting magazine my mother had left there from her stay in LA last month.

Fister was to be the vessel. He prepared by unbuttoning his shirt, then shrugging out of his tank top undershirt. As he did, he shot Victoria a sly wink while Henry was occupied pulling up wikipedia on his mother's iphone. Then, he shucked off his cargo shorts and hopped onto my guest bed clad only in his boxer briefs.

He'd been working out, I could tell. He had the faint outline of a six-pack, and bigger biceps than I'd ever seen on him. Fucker. I probably could have spent more time at the gym too if I hadn't had a silly thing like a medical practice to pay attention to. I gauged Victoria's reaction: she made a show of feigning being unimpressed, but she did sneak a second peek. She gestured to him to lie down on the bed. Fister did, and she cuffed each of his wrists to the bedposts. Then, she turned to me. "Got any rope? We should tie his legs, too."

"In the closet," Fister said.

Victoria followed his directions, and pulled a length of white rope out from my closet in the spare bedroom. I shook my head, resolving to do a thorough inspection of my condo for any unwanted items the next time Fister housesat for me.

Victoria tied Fister's legs to the bedpost, and when she had him pretty well immobilized, she turned to her son. "All right," she said. "Now what?"

Henry held the phone up and began to read out

an incantation that sounded like a mix of Latin and something else I couldn't identify. I frowned. What was it that gave these words such power?

"Just a second," Victoria said. She grabbed him by the shoulders and physically turned him around so that he was facing away from Fister.

"Mom!" Henry protested.

"There's no reason for you to watch this," Victoria said. "You can speak the power phrases just as easily facing away from the bed."

"Actually," Fister said, "Mikey's got great technique. He could learn a thing or—" Victoria glared him into submission, and he finished with a lame, "Just saying."

Once Victoria had won this battle, she turned to me. "You'd better get ready," she said to me.

I spread my hands helplessly. "What do I do?"

"You know." She mimed a jacking motion with her fist.

"Oh. Right." Grimacing, I knelt down beside the bed, next to Fister.

He looked over to me and caught my gaze. "Be gentle," he said.

"Not a chance. I owe you one, remember?"

His eyes widened. "That was over fifteen years ago. Surely you've gotten over that—"

Henry cut him off as he resumed reading the bastardized Latin incantation off the iphone screen. I waited. The incantation was longish, so I began to settle onto my haunches, slightly bored. Henry droned on, his high-pitched voice cracking every so often. Poor kid. Puberty was a bitch at the best of times. This was the polar opposite of any demon summoning I ever could have imagined. I would have felt far more reassured if we'd had someone mouthing the incantation with a rich, booming basso profundo voice that bespoke power and authority, but instead we had a scratchy retiree from the Vienna Boys' Choir. I was no expert, but I imagined that demons were kind of like tweaked-out crack whores: they would submit to the dominance of their pimp daddies. But show a little weakness, and the bitches could get . . . uppity. After all, just that morning, the demon we'd vanquished in the Starbucks dungeon had scoffed at the lack of faith behind my words. No matter what, the delivery had to matter.

But Henry seemed to know what he was doing. As he rolled toward the incantation's finale, his voice rose to a crescendo. He was facing away from the bed, but he threw himself into the delivery, and soon was gesturing wildly like a Shakespearean leading man in the direction of my closet door. He practically shouted the ending of the incantation, and finished up with a truly impassioned "*Expecto patronum!*"

A moment of silence blanketed the room. Fister, who up to that point was resting on the bed with his eyes closed, bracing against the arrival of the demon spirit in his body, opened one eye. He squinted at Henry. "Expecto patronum?" he said. "Really?"

Henry shook his head in disgust. "Fuck Wikipedia," he said.

I waited, biting my lip and holding my breath. Henry waited, too. He cast a nervous glance over his shoulder to see if any change had overtaken Fister.

Victoria waited, too. She stared down at Fister. "Come on, dammit," she muttered.

"We are summoning an angraphilic eritifal demon," Henry said. He held up the phone and read from it. "It says here if it doesn't work the first time, you can strengthen the power of the incantation if everybody gets naked and dances the white elephant." He lowered the phone. "What's the white elephant?"

"That is so not happening," Victoria muttered. "I swore in college I'd never do that again."

"Wait!" I cried. "Something's happening."

I had the closest view in the house to Fister, so I was the first one to see the at first minute changes happening to him. His right hand twitched slightly, and then the twitch crawled up his entire right arm and overtook his torso, then down his legs, until various parts of his body were spasming in response to what seemed like a myriad of different stimuli. It was as if he were responding to some low level electrical current pumped throughout his body, but as I watched, the twitches intensified to full-fledged spasms, and then the spasms transmogrified into uncontrollable bucking and thrashing. I fretted that Fister would do serious damage to his handcuffed wrists or bound ankles. I looked helplessly at Victoria and Henry, who had taken advantage of the moment to turn around and look at what was transpiring on the bed. "Whoa," he said.

The fit stopped without warning. Fister's

entire body went limp, and his head lolled to the side. Had he lost consciousness? I leaned in closer to him to check his pulse . . . and at that moment, his eyes opened again.

The eyes were the telltale signs of demon possession. They'd gone all black, with no discernible difference between iris and pupil, just like the leather daddy's we'd helped earlier this morning. I looked to Henry and Victoria. Had we unwittingly summoned another Parahelix Assumptive, instead of . . .

But then Fister flashed us all a seductive grin. "Well hellooo," he said, his voice silky, like a lounge lizard, and the eerie eyes took in all three of us in quick succession. "Nice tits," he said as he sized up Victoria. Then, he looked to Henry. "Mmm. Young and succulent. And a plushy fetish besides. What's not to love? I'll give your furry tail a pulling like you won't believe, little man." Then, he looked over at me. "And a virgin," he said.

I frowned. "I'm not a virgin," I protested. I looked to Victoria, then to Henry. "Really."

The demon shrugged with Fister's body. "Close enough," he said. "Don't worry, lover, I'll pop your cherry for you."

Victoria took charge. She took a stride forward. "We summoned you for information. We have questions for you."

The demon feigned a yawn. "Nobody summons me to talk, dearie," it said. It winked at her. "Go on, take off your clothes. Give us a nice show, eh?"

"Give us information first," Victoria said.

The demon scowled. "Why should I give you information? What's in it for me?"

"A handjob," Victoria said.

"A handjob? That's it? Come on, honey. Make it at least a Black Russian."

Henry looked quizzically at his mother. "What's a Black Russian?"

"Or how about a Philadelphia facebuster?"

Victoria shrugged, unconcerned. "A handjob, or nothing. If you hadn't noticed, you're not exactly in a position to give yourself one."

The demon considered Fister's bound body. "Such a waste of good handcuffs," it muttered.

"A handjob," Victoria repeated. "Take it or leave it."

The demon considered. "Come on. At least gimme a Mexican flapjack. Please?"

"Boys," Victoria said to Henry and me, "this fucker don't wanna play. How about we leave him alone with his thoughts, hmm?" She half-turned and made as if to leave the room. "Stuck half in this plane of existence, all alone, without anyone to even lend him a hand—"

"All right," the demon said. "You win." And then, under Fister's breath, barely audible, it muttered something that sounded to me like "Prick tease."

"Wonderful." Victoria beamed. "Tell us what you know of the demon lord."

"Which demon lord? You're going to have to be more specific."

"The one getting ready to cross over

completely into our world."

"I don't have the slightest idea what you're talking about."

"You're lying. Let's go, boys."

"All right! But ya gotta gimme some sugar first."

Victoria nodded to me, as if giving me my cue.

I closed my eyes and heaved a resigned sigh. Then, gritting my teeth, I opened my eyes again and whipped down Fister's boxer briefs, exposing his—

Sonofabitch. These fuckers really were horny.

"Well?" The demon looked down at me. Seeing Fister's face looking at me with eyes gone completely black due to demon-occulted irises gave me a serious case of the willies. However, I had a job to do . . . and Fister's serious willie wasn't going to stroke itself. So, gritting my teeth, I looked away, and tugged.

"Oooh, yeah," the demon grunted. "That's it. Yeah."

"Hey. Talk to me." Victoria snapped her fingers in the demon's face to get his attention.

"But talking is so boring. Why don't you come on over here and play with my nipples, honey?"

Victoria shook her head, as if she were dealing with a stubborn child. She looked to me. "Ball flick. Now."

I could only look at her askance.

"You know." She took her thumb and middle finger and mimed a flicking motion, like you might do to someone's forehead if they were annoying you.

"Oh." Now we were talking. I repeated the motion and applied the flick to Fister's nuts. The demon yipped in response.

"Come on," Victoria said. "Flick it like you mean it."

Grimacing, I repeated the flick. This time the demon in Fister's body thrashed against its bonds. "Hey! That effin hurt!"

"Information," Victoria repeated. "That was the deal. Tell us what we want to know, and my associate here will give you a handjob you'll never forget."

The demon grinned. "Ooh, you are kinky. I like you."

Victoria leaned forward over the bed. "Tell me the name of the demon lord."

"All right all right." The demon cocked its head to me. "Well go on. Stroke."

With a sigh, I returned to my original hand motion.

After a moment, the demon sighed contentedly. "It's Lyle."

"'Lyle?'" Victoria said. "The demon lord's name is Lyle?"

"That's his nickname. Even Lyle got tired of giving his full title every time he introduces himself. Crusher of Worlds, Destroyer of Souls, Mutilator of the Ninth Order, Scourge of Babies, that sort of thing. You know. Don't tell him I told you this, but he's a real windbag."

"I see. So who is it that's helping to incarnate him here on Earth? He must have human help to be that close to crossing over into our realm."

"Yeah. Lyle's the best. He got the biggest group of assholes on the planet."

"Who? Congress?"

"Worse."

"The Vatican?"

"Even worse than that."

"Who, then?"

"Faster."

Victoria frowned. "Pardon?"

"Not you, sweetie. Him."

I started. "Oh. Sorry." I looked questioningly to Victoria.

"Go ahead and give him what he wants," she said. "But don't let him cum until we've gotten everything we need out of him."

"Come on and bounce on my cock and I'll give you everything you could possibly need, snookums," the demon said to Victoria.

"*Who*?" Victoria demanded. A slight note of exasperation entered her voice.

Victoria gave me the signal to flick again. I readied my fingers . . .

"I dare not speak their name!" the demon protested. "All I know is they're a bunch of uptight righteous celibate fucksticks from Hell on Earth."

"Hell on Earth?" Victoria frowned. "You're going to have to put it in our terms, I'm afraid."

"Fine. What do you call it?" The demon scrunched up his face in concentration and rattled Fister's right wrist inside its handcuffs as if to urge on his memory. "Kansas, I think."

"Uptight righteous celibate fucksticks from Kansas?" I mused. "That doesn't exactly narrow it down much."

"We need a little more to go on."

"I don't know any more."

"Blue balls," Victoria instructed me. "Now."

I took my hand from Fister's shaft. I held up both my hands to show the demon that I was finished with my ministrations.

"I don't know what you humans call them," the demon said defensively. "All I know is that they show up at your human funerals and piss people off . . ."

"The Westboro Baptist Church?" Victoria asked.

"Yes! Yes, that's it!"

Victoria whistled. "Those are some uptight righteous fucksticks, all right. Lyle's going hardcore, I take it. When are they planning for him to cross over?"

"Let me finish. I'm almost there."

"Just a few more questions. Then you can cum."

"All right." The demon sighed. "It's today."

"Today?"

"That's what I just said. At least, I think it's today. You humans' reckoning of time is so infantile."

Victoria looked to her son. "You got that?" she said.

"I'm on it." Henry already had the cell phone up to his face and was typing in a search with both thumbs.

"All right. Where?"

"How the hell should I know? I'm not Lyle's

secretary."

"Where?" Victoria repeated sternly.

"I—I—I—"

I looked in concern down at the demon. At first I was wondering why it was stuttering. But then, when I saw Fister's toes curling and his back arching, I realized.

"I got it!" Henry cried. "The Westboro Baptist Church. They actually have a schedule of protests on their website." He frowned and looked up from the iphone screen. "Dude. Did you know their website is actually Godhatesfags dot com? What a bunch of fucks."

"Where is it, Henry? Where are they going to be today?"

"*Aaaiiiiieeeeee! Oh yeeeeeeaaaaaahhhhh!*" The demon spasmed, and shot a load so massive, with such force, that it splattered audibly on the ceiling.

"Dude!" Henry exclaimed. "That was friggin awesome. I so got that on video."

I looked up in disbelief at Fister's ejaculate on my ceiling—

"Henry, where are they going to be today?" Victoria's voice cut into my utter stupefaction at witnessing the most legendary cumshot I would likely ever see.

"Oh. Sorry. San Diego. They're going to be in San Diego."

—just as a glob of Fister's seed dropped from the ceiling right into my eye. I shrieked and fell backward.

And my eye burned, *burned*, with all the

searing intensity of hellfire. I clawed at my eye, as if clawing it out would be preferable to that horrible, hideous sensation of flames lodged behind my cornea.

Victoria was over me in an instant. She firmly gripped my hands to keep them away from my face. "Look at me!" she said. "Look at me!" I don't know how many times she repeated herself, but eventually her cool, insistent voice penetrated the single-minded blaze of perception occasioned by my burning eye.

First I forced open my unaffected eye. Then, after several moments of eyelid spasms, I was able to blink open the eye that had taken Fister's demon splooge—

Henry had joined his mother and was peering over her shoulder at me. Both of them recoiled in shock.

"What?" I said. "What is it?"

"Dude," Henry said, "Your eye's red."

"Of course it's red! A demon just came in my eye!"

"No, I mean . . . it's like . . . really red."

I stared at them in horror. Then, I found my feet and stumbled toward the guest bathroom. I batted at the light switch and stumbled over to the mirror over the sink.

I peered at myself in the mirror.

Henry was right. My right eye was red. I mean completely, demonically red. Pulsating. Like a fucking stop light where my pupil should have been.

CHAPTER FIVE

"It's probably only temporary," Henry said as we rode in his mother's back seat on the interstate toward San Diego. "I wouldn't worry about it. It'll probably go away."

"Probably?" I said. "How do you know? Has a demon ever cum in your eye before?" We'd only been in the car twenty minutes or so, but it was long enough for me to entertain gruesome visions of what the demon seed could do to me. Would a demon fetus take root in my ocular nerve and explode fully formed from my eye at some inopportune moment? Or worse, would the seed fester in my eye socket like batshit acid and slowly turn my entire face into a mess of rot?

"It wasn't really demon cum," Fister said. He was riding in the front seat. I was not particularly relieved to see that he seemed to be completely free of the demon infestation. While I'd scrubbed and scrubbed at my burning eye in the bathroom sink, Henry had spoken the incantation to banish the demon back to the horny depths of hell. "It was really just my cum, tainted a little by the demon."

"Great," I muttered. "That makes me feel *so* much better."

"Is it still burning?" Henry asked.

"A little," I said. The intense burning sensation had subsided a little, but it was still there, licking at the tendrils of my optic nerve, simmering . . .

"Let me see it," Henry said.

I took off the sunglasses I'd hastily grabbed on the way out the door. I scrunched closed my good eye. Henry leaned in a little closer and peered into the infected one.

"Well?" I prompted.

"Dude, that is so badass," Henry said.

"It's still red, then?"

"Oh yeah."

"Can't you find anything on Wikipedia about getting rid of it?"

"I looked."

"And?"

"Well . . . there are a couple of methods for getting rid of demonic growths. But they're pretty drastic. We probably don't wanna cut out your eyeball just yet. But hey. Look on the bright side."

"There's a bright side?"

"Yeah." He grinned. "If we do end up having to cut out your eyeball, at least you've got two doctors who can do it for you."

"A gynecologist and a proctologist," I said. "Great. One asshole, and one twat."

"Look, I'm sorry," Fister said. "It's not like I can really control where my cum lands at the best of times. And this time, I wasn't even in control of my own body."

"Look," Victoria, in the driver's seat, cut in, "you'll be fine, so stop whining about it already, would you? Just let us know if anything starts licking your eyeball."

"*What*? Licking?"

"I'm really far more concerned about what we're gonna do when we get to San Diego. If traffic holds up we'll be there in under two hours, and we need a plan."

"All right," Fister said. "What do we know?"

Henry consulted his phone. "The church is planning on picketing outside of Triton Stadium."

"What's the event being held there?" Fister asked.

"Looks like it's qualifying rounds for the Special Olympics," Henry said. He looked up from his phone. "Yeesh. That's pretty cold, even for these motherfuckers."

"Henry, language!"

"Sorry, mom."

"So these guys almost always draw counter-protesters," I said. "Usually even larger crowds. We could just get the crowd to run them off—"

"Not a bad idea," Fister said, "but it would only postpone the problem. The church members would still be infested with demons. There's nothing to stop them from regrouping somewhere less public. Somewhere we wouldn't necessarily be able to find them."

"So that's a problem," Henry said. "We've gotta perform a mass exorcism. Maybe twenty or more of them. At the same time. They're not just gonna lie down and wait patiently while we anoint their assholes one at a time.

"Are there other ways of banishing demons?" I asked.

"Yeah, but they're generally even messier."

"Messier how?"

"Well, if we had a flamethrower we could burn the bodies to a crisp. When the vessel dies, the demons would have to be evicted back to their own realm."

"Except we're fresh out of flamethrowers," Fister said. "Not to mention that I'd kind of like to *not* be tried for mass murder if at all possible."

We tossed around idea after idea as we inched closer and closer to San Diego. Most of our ideas were impractical or impossible to implement—since we didn't really have access to things like a twenty-headed dildo or a flamethrower or enough archbishop semen to load into a SuperSoaker water pistol. Ultimately, we all came back to just one idea:

"We're gonna have to incite the crowd of counter-protesters to beat the living shit out of these guys," Fister summarized for us. "It shouldn't be too hard. I mean, these guys really are assholes."

"Yeah, but am I correct in assuming that for this to really work, the crowd is going to have to really kill them? Anything less would fail to banish the demons inside, right?"

"Yeah," Fister said.

"Is that really . . . can we really do that? Ethically, I mean? Would we really be any better than the church members who conjured the demons in the first place?"

"Sacrifice twenty menaces to society in order to save thousands of lives?" Victoria mused. "I suppose I could live with that."

"Yeah, but . . ." I looked over at Henry. "What about your son? Do you really want him to be a murderer at thirteen?"

"We don't need to murder anybody," Fister pointed out. "We'll get the crowd to do it for us."

"That's a technicality. Ultimately, the responsibility—"

"We've had two hours to come up with a better idea," Victoria said. "We didn't. It's too late. We're here."

She pulled her Azera to a stop in one of the parking garages at UC San Diego. I felt my heart thud in my throat as she shut off the vehicle: this was it. My eye pulsated rhythmically, as if in anticipation.

We got out of the car. "Which way to the stadium?" Fister asked. He cast about looking for signs.

"This way," I said. And without bothering to see if they were following me, I started walking in the direction of Triton Stadium.

Fister fell into step behind me, followed closely by Henry and his mother. "Mikey?" Fister said, concerned. "Mikey, are you all right?"

"Fine," I grunted.

"How did you know which way to the stadium? You're shit at directions, remember?"

"I—I just know." And even now, I still just knew. The throbbing of my eye was pointing me unerringly in the direction of the stadium, like a divining rod for demons. I felt—no, I *knew*—instinctively, that there were demons ahead of us.

From the parking garage to the stadium was a short hike. We could have found the site by flowing in the direction of the most people alone, but as we drew nearer the pulsating in my eye grew more and more intense. It was like my very own Spidey sense, and although one part of me realized that it was directing me toward the biggest motherfucking knot of demons I'd ever seen—hell, I'd never seen *any* demons before this morning, much less a whole clusterfuck of them—but another part of me was propelled forward, against all sense, by some unholy compulsion.

And with no warning, I farted. A real juicy jockeys-stainer of a rip. Yeah, that was gonna leave a mark.

"Christ, Mikey, did you have to?" Fister, who was walking just downwind of me, waved his hand in front of his nose. "Man, that's fucking rank."

"At least I waited until we were out of the car," I pointed out.

Fister let it drop. At that moment, we came upon the site of the Westboro Baptist Church's protest. They were clustered in a group outside and off to the side of the entrance to the stadium. There were maybe a score of them, all men, as far as I could see, and they held a variety of handmade picket signs.

HANDICAPPED CHILDREN ARE YOUR PUNISHMENT FOR LOVING FAGS
read one.

BROKEN MORALS, BROKEN BABIES

read another.   And of course, the most ubiquitous message, in all its simplicity:

GOD HATES FAGS.

I frowned.   I wondered briefly what kind of deficit of logic it would take to equate faggotry with the occurrence of handicapped children, but then I supposed hatred was never really logical. These were, after all, the people whom even a demon had professed to be the biggest assholes in the world.   How ironic that they professed to have the love of Jesus in their hearts while at the same time their assholes were flaming with the demon-infested reek of sulphur.

The entire air smelt of it.   It must have been off-putting to the small crowd of counter-protesters, because they kept their distance, separated by a token trio of police officers who stood in the no-man's land between the two groups to keep the peace.   I was dismayed by the size of the group: perhaps only a dozen people had shown up to counter-protest the church's message.

GOD LOVES EVERYBODY

read one of their signs, which was hand-decorated with a rainbow flag.

HATE SHALL NOT PREVAIL

read another one.   It was this one to which my eyes were drawn.   Under other circumstances, it might have been an uplifting message, but now, seeing just how outnumbered were the people we were depending upon to dispel this protest, I began to despair.

Fister, Henry, and Victoria realized it, too.

They drew up behind me and stared. "That's not going to be enough," Henry said.

"Maybe . . . maybe if we . . . there's a whole audience inside the stadium," Fister said. But his reasoning trailed off; there was no readily apparent way of getting an audience of people from *inside* the stadium to storm *outside* for the express purpose of kicking some douchebags' asses. What was wrong with America? What ever happened to good ol'-fashioned moral outrage?

But we weren't to have that chance. As the four of us drew up short at the head of the passel of counter-protesters, we drew the attention of the Westboro church members. Across the distance separating us, they started to become agitated. One of them pointed at us—

—and then all score or so of them linked arms and formed one giant Red Rover line of death. The demons inhabiting their bodies were on blatant display: their eyes, to a man, glowed a demonic red.

And as one, they cackled, an unholy, screeching sound to rend every last shred of hope from the soul. "Welcome, demon hunters!" cried one in the middle, pointing at us. "You're just in time for the fun to begin!" And they collapsed again into peals of giggles.

Their appearance was beginning to unnerve the meager mass of counter-protesters behind us. I could sense the group's resolve crumbling in the face of this unnatural threat.

"Yes!" the spokesman acknowledged the counter-protesters' lack of resolve. "Run for your miserable lives, and live. Stay here, and you will perish in the flames of purification!"

On cue, the entire line of church members whipped off their pants in one fluid motion, like they'd all worn easy-release stripper pants just for this occasion. Then, they turned around, bent over . . .

. . . and let rip. As one, twenty assholes erupted in jets of green-tinged flames. The three police officers in the middle were directly in the trajectory; they were instantly immolated, and their shrieks of pain and terror overrode the church members' unholy cackling for several seemingly interminable moments.

The counter-protesters' resolve completely crumbled then. They shrieked in fright and bolted, leaving only the four of us to face off against an entire squadron of the demon-infested.

The jets of flame died down even as the police officers' flaming bodies clawed their last, futile motions out on the pavement and collapsed. Still in the throes of their unholy synchronization, the church members straightened and turned around to address us, their demon-swelled boners on flagrant display.

"It is meet that you have come, demon hunters," the group's mouthpiece said in a voice that was at once sepulchral and nasally at the same time. "For the most holy of demon lords will be born amidst the flames, and his first feast shall be upon your despair!"

And his cohorts erupted in an orgy of cackling that sounded like the chittering of a whole fuckload of chimpanzees.

"But wait!" The mouthpiece held up his hand, and the satanic guffawing ceased. "What's this?" The man sniffed the air. "Did you bring us one more for His ascension?"

"One more?" Fister mumbled. "What the fuck's he talking—"

"Me," I said. I took off my sunglasses, revealing my pulsating red eye. "He's talking about me." And to add punctuation to my words, an unholy fart ripped out of my anus, accompanied by a tiny plume of green flames that ripped the seat out of both my underwear and pants at the same time.

I looked to Fister, then to Victoria, and then to Henry. "I—I'm sorry," I said. "It's getting harder and harder to resist." I gestured to my eye. "It's . . . He's calling out to me."

"Mikey, no. You can't," Fister said. "You've got to fight—"

"No," I said. "He's right. You can't win."

And I left them there, gaping, and I crossed the distance separating me from the church members, conscious of Fister's crestfallen gaze of utter betrayal at my back.

As I melded into their line, the demon-possessed church members erupted in a raucous shout, like spectators at a football match, made all the more ominous by the sepulchral tones to their voices from their otherworldly inhabitants. I joined in, giving vent to the demonic impulses swirling inside me. My eye was pulsating, but moreover, as my proximity to my brethren demon-possessed increased, my entire body felt as if it was thrumming with a current of power that was calling out to be released.

And no sooner had I arrived than the entire line rushed forward, fanning out to cut off the retreat of my friends. The church members, with me in their midst, moved as one to encircle the three. And then, I and all twenty-one of my brethren closed ranks, tightening our circle so there could be no escape.

"Mikey?" Fister said, and his voice, normally so confident, actually quavered. He sounded more like Henry than himself. "Mikey, help us. Please. I know you're still in there."

His words triggered a cacophonous guffaw in unison from the entire congregation. "He is with us now!" their mouthpiece exulted as their mirth died down. "Your deaths will be fitting, demon hunters, as you have caused the demises of so many of our brethren. He will cross over among the flames, and His first feast in this world will be upon your bones."

And then, all twenty-one of us turned around in unison and crouched, aiming our anuses directly toward the center of the circle, where the incipient blast of hellfire would scorch them completely. They'd burn. They'd burn, exactly like the three hapless police officers before them. And I could feel the hellfire kindling in my entire body, as surely as it must be in the entire rest of the congregation. It was roiling and burbling inside me and crying out for release. Soon . . . soon . . .

"Mikey!" Fister cried. "You can't do this! Please!" He was now huddled on the ground with Victoria and Henry both, crouched, as if that could save them from the cleansing blast of hellfire that was soon to come.

I paid them no heed. I looked instead to my brethren, the demon-possessed around me. As we waited for the hellfire to crescendo inside our bodies, they all joined hands. I looked down to my left, at the hand of the man who'd taken my hand. Then, I looked to the man on the right. Both, with their pants long since blazed to smithereens right off their bums, and their tiny erections sticking straight up in the air like a salute for the arrival of their master. All around the circle, the story was the same. The collection of rock-hard liver-spotted cocks all stood at attention, pointing straight out before them like spikes on a great wheel.

God, what a bunch of fags.

Ironic, wasn't it, that the group who claimed to hate fags the most was awaiting the arrival of their lord by standing hand-in-hand with their brethren and sporting raging boners.

And I realized I wasn't hard in the slightest. Whatever kinship my body and my slight case of demon possession might have felt with these people ended at my midriff. Really, these guys just didn't do it for me. I didn't have a boner for the arrival of Lyle.

Which meant that in all likelihood, neither did they. The boners were all theirs. Their human hosts, I mean.

"Mikey!" Fister cried one more time.

"Fuck you!" I sneered.

The congregation chortled. "Yeah!" The mouthpiece echoed my sentiment. "Fuck you!"

"Fuck you, you faggots!" I continued, pitching my voice to rise above the ripple of chortles that echoed all along the line of congregants.

"*Faggots!*" my brethren chanted behind me.

"Filthy, disgusting faggots! Lyle is coming, and all faggots will be cleansed from the Earth!" I cried.

"*Cleansed!*" my brethren echoed.

"For when he arrives," I continued in my best televangelist's voice, "He will judge the faggots by their own wickedness. He's gonna fuck all the faggots!"

"*Fuck the faggots!*" my brethren echoed.

"Fuck the faggots!" I cried louder.

"*Fuck the faggots!*" The congregation responded to my oratory.

"*Fuck the faggots!*" I cried at the top of my lungs. I mimed thrusting motions with my hips. "*Fuck the faggots!*" The congregation, carried by my invective, did likewise. All around the circle, all twenty members began thrusting violently in echo of me.

"When Lyle is risen, he shall plug their vile assholes. He shall do unto them as they have done to each other. *Fuck the faggots!*"

"Fuck the faggots!" the congregation shouted.

They were mine. "Fuck the faggots *now!*" I cried. And I turned ninety degrees to the left. As one, they all followed my lead.

I mimed one last hip-thrust. And then I dived out of the circle.

Just in time. I rolled to a stop and watched as every member of the circle penetrated their brother in front of them. In the heat of their frenzy each of them thrust his cock into his neighbor's asshole, creating a perfect daisy chain of copulation among the score of congregants.

The timing was right. The hellfire burbled to a crescendo and ripped out of their anuses. But instead of being directed at Fister, Henry, and Victoria at the center of their circle, it was stymied by every plugged asshole. Caught in the throes of their butt-fucking, the church members didn't even realize there was a problem as the hellfire they'd cooked up inside them for so long had no avenue for release. Instead of jetting out, the hellfire exploded in a massive flash of green, ripping the church members' bodies apart into clumps of flesh that flew in all directions.

I shielded myself from the rain of gore as best I could. It was a mostly futile attempt: twenty bodies exploding produced *a fuckload* of ick.

When it finally subsided, I still kept my head tucked into my arms, afraid to look up. An eerie silence settled over the entire scene.

And then: "Eeeeewwww."

It was Henry. Cautiously, I lifted my head. I looked over to where the center of the circle had been.

Henry, Victoria, and Fister still huddled, clutching each other. They looked like utter shit, caked as they were by blood and viscera. But they were alive.

They were alive.

I got to my feet. And I ran to them. Stumblingly, I made my way across the slippery parking lot of gore. And I joined their bear hug, and for a second we remained like that, locked in our own private embrace, utterly heedless of the dripping mess of shit we'd been baptized in.

At length, we all drew back. We looked at each other. And then, unbidden, we all laughed. It was a sound of pure relief and joy and exaltation all mixed into one.

"You did it, Mikey!" Fister said at length. "You figured out how to plug twenty assholes all at once. You're a genius!"

I shrugged. "It was pretty obvious, really. Who else but a bunch of pathetically repressed queers would profess to hate fags so much?"

"I knew you'd never go over to them," Henry said.

"Your eye," Victoria said. "It's . . ."

I blinked experimentally once, twice. "Is it back to normal?"

"Well . . . sort of."

I didn't have a chance to press her for further details. Fister turned to survey the scene of Lyle's destruction. "What now?" he said. "What do we do now?"

We all basked in a moment of companionable silence as we contemplated the import of what we'd just accomplished. For this one moment, this one brief moment . . . we knew the most important thing of all:

We'd saved the world.

It was Henry who finally answered Fister's semi-rhetorical question: "I think I'm gonna hurl," he said.

EPILOGUE

We came back together at my apartment, after long, long showers filled with furious scrubbing.

"What now?" Fister asked the question that was on all our minds. He looked to Henry, then to Victoria, then to me. "We can't just go back to the old way of doing things, can we? Lone rangers, known only as avatars over the internet?"

Henry shrugged. He'd discarded his honey badger costume. He looked ridiculous in one of my T-shirts that hung huge on his lanky frame. "We make a pretty good team, you know," he said. "We should . . ." He faltered. He looked questioningly to his mother, who was staring off into space.

She'd been paying attention to the conversation, though. "We should be a team," she said.

"Why not?" Fister said. "There's always going to be demons. And the world has plenty of assholes."

They all three looked at me expectantly.

I shrugged. "Why not?" I said. "Let's be a team."

They grinned in unison.

"Only—"

Their grins went on hiatus.

"Only we've gotta come up with another name," I said. "Demon ass whuppers just sounds really . . . gay."

"How about 'demon busters?'" Fister suggested. "You know, like Ghostbusters?"

Victoria shook her head. "Nah. Too eighties."

"How about the Demon Exterminators?" Henry suggested.

I shook my head. "How about something without 'demons' in it? I don't want the whole world to think we're psycho."

Fister chuckled. "What about 'The Psycho Proctologists?'"

"I'm not a proctologist," Victoria pointed out. "I'm a gynecologist."

"We can't help it if you're a twat," Fister said.

"Well, that would make you a butthole," Victoria threw back.

"I know you are, but what am I?"

"I like it," Henry piped up.

Victoria glared at him. "Traitor."

"Hey," Henry spread his hands as if to indicate his innocence, "I bet you nobody owns the domain name."

I chuckled. "Well, you've probably got a point there, kiddo." And I winked at him.

With my third eye. With my other two—the normal ones—I surveyed our newly minted team. And I thought that it was good.

AUTHOR'S AFTERWARD

My dearest sick fucks,

If you've read this far, then I congratulate you. Your fortitude is legendary.

Psycho Proctologists and the Flaming Buttholes of Doom was written mostly on a lark while I was under deadline to write something else under a different pen name. Now that I finally got it out of my system, I can let it rest.

Except Mikey, Fister, Victorian, and Henry the Nasty-Ass Honey Badger keep pestering me. I think there's another little book about their exploits inside me somewhere just waiting for me to ejaculate it onto the page (ewwww . . . sorry about that mental image).

If you're as sick a fuck as I am, and you would like to see *Psycho Proctologists #2: Hakuna Matata, Vagina Dentata,* then please take a moment to encourage me in my madness.

Vist my youtube channel, where you can see homemade book trailers:

www.youtube.com/psychoproctologists

Or on facebook:

www.facebook.com/psychoproctologists

Or drop by the Psycho Proctologists blog and leave a comment:

www.psychoproctologists.blogspot.com

I'd love to hear about your reactions to *Psycho Proctologists and the Flaming Buttholes of Doom.* I'd even love to hear if you absolutely loathed the book . . . because if you hated this book that much, then what the fuck are you doing reading this far, you butthole?

Sincerely,
W.W. Pecker